The Lasting Gift

Translated by Anu Raj Joshi

Translator's Note

This poetic fiction, in the form of free verses, is a loose translation of Satya Mohan Joshi's poetry entitled **Nepal-ya Rastriye Bibhuti Kalakar Arniko-ya Sweta Chaitya** published by Nepal Bhasa Parishad in 1984.

It is based on the true story of Arniko (1244-1306), a Nepalese who crossed the Himalayas more than 700 years ago and designed and built the White Dagoba in Beijing. Designated as a historical treasure after the founding of the People's Republic of China, this Dagoba, is open to tourists.

The readers will experience as if listening to a tourist guide telling a curious story in broken language. Some unusual terms explained in glossary chapter at the end will be informative to tourists as well.

The glossary is tailored mainly from the original book. Bibliography is at the end.

Spelling of proper nouns in this book may not be correct or consistent due to different sources.

Sincere thanks to all responsible personalities affiliated with Nepal Bhasa Parishad, Bibliography, TRAFFORD and everyone concerned directly or indirectly in the preparation and publication of this book.

Anu Raj Joshi
138/39 Sri Ganesh Marg, Tahachal, Kathmandu, Nepal
zocyalpha@gmail.com
November 7, 2007

 www.trafford.com
North America & international
toll-free: 1 888 232 4444 (USA & Canada)
fax: 812 355 4082

Bright full moon is shining.
Colorful flowers are blooming.
Fair breeze is blowing.
Da Du's environment is cool, peaceful and amusing.

The whole town is so lively.
Every house is decorated very nicely.

Seasonal fruits, beans and soybeans,
Specially cooked Yue Ye Ping and cereals,
Are displayed as offerings,
To Chang Ah with devotions.

Sweet smell from burning incense sticks filled the air.
Jung Chew Jie festival is being celebrated in a grand manner.

Nicely dressed children are singing and dancing.
The parents are calling— "Children! Come, have sweets!"

Semi-drunk grand parents are raising their voice—
"Hurry up kids!
It's time to tell the story of Mother Chang Ah,
Who reached the moon carrying elixir-wine."

xxx

Seated inside the imperial palace,
On a colorful throne decorated with dragons,
Is Emperor Hu Pi Le, the founder of Yuan Dynasty.

Greeting him on the occasion of the Jung Chew Jie festival are—
The empresses, the princesses and the princes,
And the people gathered down the dais.

A messenger came bowing and reported—
"Your Majesty, Teacher Pasapa has arrived.
A gentleman from Nepal is with him."

Curiosity prevailed.
Everyone eyed towards the arrival side.

Some whispered audibly—
"A gentleman from Nepal?
What could be the good reason that he is here?"

Miao Yen asked—
"Papa, where is Nepal situated?
Any idea why he is here?"

The emperor answered—
"South of Tibet it lies.
Lumbini, the birthplace of Lord Buddha, is there.
So it is said.
But I don't know why he is here."

xxx

Pasapa greeted the emperor.
The courteous gentleman also greeted.
Everybody's attention gravitated towards the youth from Nepal.

The emperor offered the teacher a seat beside.
The teacher asked the youth to sit next beside.

Having exchanged few words of well-being,
The teacher began to present the foreigner—

"Your Majesty, I beg you to listen.
By grace of Your Majesty,
Construction of Golden Stupa in Tibet is complete.
It is marvelous.

"This gentleman was the team leader.
He is very skilled and hardworking.
I took him here as a disciple-friend of mine.
'Cause, skillful persons like him are not to be found in millions.
He too has shown interest in seeing places."

The audience stood puzzling.
Miao Yen's innocent eyes started deepening.
Ashamed of excess admiration, Arniko stood bowing.

The emperor inquired—
"Gentleman,
You came here instead of returning to your own country,
After completing your assignment in Tibet.
Any special reason?"

Nervous Arniko glanced at the teacher.

Pasapa gestured—
"Don't get nervous. Be frank."

Encouraged, Arniko began to talk.
"Your Majesty, I have two reasons to come here.
First reason—
It is said that,
Lord Buddha's tooth is preserved somewhere in this country.
I wish to pay a visit there.
And have a glance of it.

"Second reason—
It is told,
The big monastery of Maha Manjushree who came to Nepal,
Also lies in this very country near the Five Sister Mountains.
I wish to go there on pilgrimage.
And pay homage."

xxx

Arniko's noble spirit impressed all.

An old courtier broke the silence—
"Oh yes!
I, too, have paid a visit there and seen that sacred tooth.
It is nicely exhibited in a reliquary inside an octagonal pagoda,
Near Pa Da Chu Monastery."

Another old man, a religious pundit,
Recollected his memory and spoke—
"Five Sister Mountains should be the Wu Thai San.

"I remember,
During my childhood, it was told—
Lord Manjushree had set out for Nepal from there.
I came to know now,
That was a true story."

xxx

The emperor is in consultation with Pasapa.
Miao Yen could not help her eyes flirting, towards the stranger.
Arniko himself is looking serious.
He is anxiously expecting the emperor's comments.

The emperor urged—
"Well, gentleman!
Since you have already arrived here,
Crossing the very Jhomolongmo Himalayas,
You may get settled in this very country.

"No doubt, your wishes shall be fulfilled."

Arniko could not speak.
He was overwhelmed by the remembrance of Nepal.

In the meantime, Miao Yen queried—
"Papa, how far is Nepal from here?"

Without waiting the answer,
She once again happened to look at Arniko.
This time, her eyes fell on the wedding ring on his finger.

The emperor in his turn signaled an old minister,
To furnish answers to Miao Yen's query.

The old minister gently stroked his head with his right hand,
Closed the eyes for a moment and came up with this answer—
"Nepal lies southwest from here and is ten thousand Li away."

Listening this, she entered into a world of her own imagination.
And, she wondered on Nepal's whereabouts.

Arniko was told—
"Gentleman, take your time and decide yourself.
But, for the time being, I want to bother you with a problem.
You have to repair an image."

Quickly, the emperor ordered a minister in front of him—
"Get the image!"

Soon, the image was brought.

The emperor said—
"Gentleman,
This image I liked best has been a gift from Emperor Sung.
Unfortunately, it slipped down and broke into pieces.

"I wonder,
With your skills, you might be able to repair it."

Arniko, inspected the image carefully.
And, prayed the God of Skills silently.

Next moment, the emperor asked—
"Do you think you can repair it perfectly?"

Arniko replied confidently—
"Needs lots of brazing and many fine adjustments.
But, it won't be very difficult. I will repair it."

The emperor wanted to reconfirm—
"Are you sure you can repair it?"

Arniko replied—
"Your Majesty, I am a son of Nepal.
You can count on my words."

Emperor Hu Pi Le was delighted.
The others were astonished.

The truth was that—

No one ever had shown such courage to repair it.

Salient feature of this image was that—

It depicted the diagram of Zhen Ziu.

Clothed warmly in heavy winter clothes,
Pasapa and Arniko are riding on the same course.

Cold northerly wind is blowing.
Ditches and ponds are frozen.
Trees are without any leaf.
Passers-by are rarely in sight.

Before dark, they reached a small settlement.
There, they encountered some children playing snowballs.

Pasapa suggested—
"Tonight we shall stop over at this place."

Arniko acknowledged— "Alright."

Pointing towards the west, Pasapa said—
"Look at the forest hill over there!
Shao Sin Temple is protruding.
That's the temple where the sacred tooth is kept."

The top portion of the temple was sighted.
Prayed 'Namo Ratna Trayayo!' and remarked—
"That should be a pagoda style temple.
Am I right?"

Pasapa smiled and replied—
"Yes, Arniko Dear, you are so sharp!"

Both Pasapa and Arniko turned towards their ponies,
That started growling.
They noticed some children running away,
After pulling out hair from their tails.

Lodged in a little cottage,
Pasapa and Arniko went to bed straight after eating.
Soon, both of them fell asleep on Kang's.

But, the owner of the cottage, an old lady, is still awake.
She is boiling some water for a cup of tea.

About midnight,
Arniko is woken up by the ponies tethered under a tree.
They were complaining against the snow.

He headed to open the door.
But the old lady interrupted— "Don't open! It's snowfall again!"

He slowly raised the curtain and peeped out of the window.
The brown ponies were turning white.

He became restless.
He could not sleep any more.
He thought this and that.

"What a snowfall!
Snowfall around Five Sister Mountains would be even heavier.
Probably, Pasapa won't take me there this winter."

Next moment, he thought about the scroll he saw,
In the meeting room inside the palace.

It had the portrait of Maha Manjushree,
Seated in divinely position,
On the top of a huge lotus flower, over the back of a lion.

The morning broke.
The ponies were fed.
After breakfast, they rode uphill heading towards Pa Da Chu.

Trees looked as if having silver skins.
The vast field extending beyond Da Du metropolis,
Looked as if it was a sea of molten silver.

Hours later, they arrived at the beginning of a stairway.
They climbed the stairs to the entrance of a monastery.
A group of monks welcomed them.

Black tea was served after being seated.
In the process of briefing, Pasapa introduced Arniko—
"I have good news. This gentleman is Arniko from Nepal.

"He was the leader of the team,
For the construction of Golden Stupa in Tibet.

"Our Emperor asked him to repair an image,
He did it perfectly.
It looked even better than before.

"The Emperor is so pleased with his skills,
He appointed him Chief of the Department of Handicrafts."

An old monk commented—
"Oh! It is in fact very good news.
Nepal happens to have such skilled artists."

Another monk, absorbed in Pasapa's words, urged—

"Please continue."

Pasapa added—
"This gentleman is a practical follower of Buddhism.
He can fluently recite prayers like—
Namsangiti, Pragyaparmita Hridayasutra, Pancha Rachha, etc.

"He is also capable to explain what he knows,
Clearly, in a simple way."

The same monk expressed—
"Then, we are having an opportunity,
To exchange our views on different topics."

Embarrassed, Arniko began to speak—
"Honorable Monks, I know some basics only."

The monk comforted him—
"Arniko Dear,
No one is perfect in this world.
It is said that even Gods have to keep on trying,
To reach perfection."

xxx

Mahasthavir, the chief of the monastery,
Escorted Arniko into Shao Sin Temple.

There, he opened a container made of stone.
Inside was a small wooden reliquary.

When this reliquary was opened,
The sacred tooth of Lord Buddha came in sight.

At the very sight of the sacred tooth,
Arniko visualized heavenly rays radiating from it.
He prayed 'Namo Ratna Trayayo!'

After praying, he inspected the tooth.
He saw the caption in Ranjana script—
'Ye Dharma Hetu Prabhava,
Hetustesan Tathagatohebadat,
Tesan Cha Yo Nirodh Yebambadi Mahasrawan.'

Then he seated himself in a meditating position,
And closed his eyes for a while.

He was reminded of this—
Whatever we see,
They are grown out of nothing under certain conditions.
To be born, to get old and to be dead,
Are, but, the consequence of certain conditions.

Seeing Arniko's inclination,
Another monk, a taller one, said—
"At the time Lord Buddha's soul departed after Nirvana,
Only two molars remained out of his entire teeth.
They are called Danta Dhatu.

"One of them was taken to Sri Lanka.
The other was brought to China.

"The story is like this—
It was taken from Kusi Nagar to Udayan in India.
From Udayan, it was carried to Khotan.
From Khotan, it reached Chang An.

"Finally, from Chang An,
It was brought to Yen Ching during Liau Dynasty,
And safely preserved here.

"This place is also called Fo Ya Tho.
There are one thousand portraits of Lord Buddha in this temple."

Then, Arniko began to orbit this temple for 108 times,
Chanting 'Ye Dharma Hetu Prabhava.'

xxx

Arniko and Pasapa stayed in this monastery for some days.
Here, Arniko studied various styles of Chinese art and artifacts.
The monk-scholars helped him a lot.

In the meeting room inside the imperial palace,
Some courtiers are in consultation with Pasapa.

Suddenly, Arniko remembered his home,
And the lovely face of his wife.

He had promised her one night—
"I am leaving this country.
But, I will certainly come back."

Yes! His body is in China.
But, his mind is flying back.

At one instance, he saw the chariot of Lord Bungadyo,
Passing in front of his house in Nepal.

Unconsciously, he prayed—
"Oh Karunamaya Loknath,
Please rescue all the beings!"

xxx

Miao Yen arrived attended by young maids.
Arniko's memories dissipated.

After a while, Emperor Hu Pi Le arrived followed by bodyguards.
Everybody greeted him very warmly.

He told Pasapa—
"Teacher, today, I need your advice."

Pasapa said—
"Your Majesty, please go ahead."

14

Next, the emperor asked his daughter—
"You told me, you have some questions with Arniko.
Did you ask him?"

Miao Yen replied— "No. Not yet."

So, the emperor himself mentioned—
"Miao Yen wants to know something about Bhrikuti,
The daughter of Nepal."

Everybody looked at Arniko eagerly.
He prayed Mother Saraswati for a moment.
Then he began to speak cautiously.

"Frankly,
Although I am a Nepalese, I know very little about Bhrikuti.
But in Lhasa, she is worshipped as Tara.

"Buddhism, she carried, has linked China and Nepal forever.
This is what I have seen with my own eyes."

He added—
"Had ladies like Bhrikuti and Wen Chen not arrived in Lhasa,
People's mind would have been still preoccupied by ghosts.
And, in place of Potala Square,
There would have been just the hillocks sheltered by bats."

Miao Yen was absorbed in these words.
She came to know that,
Some ladies had contributed a lot for the spread of Buddhism.
She began to explore within herself.

The emperor intervened— "You still have some questions?"

She answered—
"I have one more question."

The emperor smiled and said—
"He is not returning to his country right now.
I will be giving him new assignments.
So, you may ask him many questions later."

She was happy.

xxx

The emperor drew Pasapa's attention.
He told him about his resolutions.
Both of them looked at ease.

One courtier whispered into the ear of another—
"Sure, they are not talking about any battle."

The emperor told Arniko—
"Gentleman,
I have already consulted with the Teacher.
I am giving you one new assignment.
Hope, you can realize my ambition."

Arniko responded—
"Your Majesty!"

The emperor added—
"I was and I still am determined,
To turn this deserted Chung Du into a huge capital city,
Filled with greatness of all kinds.

"So, I renamed it Da Du,
And a vast town square has been developed,
Around the Imperial Palace.

"Huge boundary walls,
With attractive gates in four directions,
Surround this square;
And beautiful ponds and parks are well maintained.

"But, I feel something still missing.

"Now, after serious consultation with the Teacher,
I came to this conclusion—
For the cause of national integrity and prosperity,
A huge, prominent and beautiful Dagoba has to be erected.

"It should be constructed in such a grand manner that,
It does saliently exhibit for ever—
Calm, cool, quiet and peaceful vastness.

"Only then,
The name Da Du, given to this capital city, will be appropriate."

Entrusted, Arniko spoke courageously with pride and honor—
"Your Majesty, I will try my best.
I will use all my skills and ideas to realize Your Majesty's wish.
Such a Dagoba shall certainly be erected."

Excited by such a warm and reliable response from Arniko,
The emperor added—
"Gentleman, I fully trust you!
Of course, your skills shall certainly be recognized and prized."

Next, the emperor said—

"Teacher,

In my dream, I saw some lighted body.

It was glowing brilliantly nearby Fu Che Men gate.

"How about erecting this huge Dagoba at this very site?"

Pasapa whole-heartedly supported the emperor—

"Your Majesty,

If it is so, that is the best site."

Trees all around the south-facing garden are completely naked.
But, some seasonal flowers are blooming in different flowerpots.

Pine and oak bonsai are nicely decorated in huge porcelain pots.
Sparrows and other birds are flying from one place to another.

Life-size dragons look real.
They are on either side of the gate sheathed in gilded metal.
'Heavenly Garden' is embossed along the arch of this very gate.

Somewhere in this garden,
On the platform called the Moonlight Stage,
The emperor is being assisted by some young maids.

One of them is combing his long hair.
Another one is pulling out grey hair.
Two others are massaging from sides either,
With oil that smelt sweeter than ever.

A black hair was pulled by mistake.
The emperor looking at the mirror,
Flew into a temper.

He gave a slap on her cheek.
And scolded violently—
"What's wrong with your eyes?
Are you turning blind?"

Terrified, she bowed down,
And tendered shamefaced apologies—
"Your Majesty, I beg your pardon.
Please excuse me."

In the meantime,
The dearest empress Wang Chung is arriving.

Her long hair almost touched the ground.
The artful movement of her two small feet,
Resembled those of swan.

Two maids followed her.

At the very sight of the dearest one,
The emperor finished his make-up in a hurry.

He stepped forward, hugged with love and inquired—
"You told you have been directing a drama.
When do you plan to stage the dress rehearsal?"

Smilingly the dearest one replied,
Raising her long dress—
"Just half done so far.
It is so easy to talk about,
But, very difficult to work as a director."

The emperor said—
"Since you yourself are directing it,
Direct it in such a way that,
It comes out praiseworthy.
Especially because,
This time, we have guests from far and abroad."

The empress reacted sourly—
"Your Majesty, I hear,
Your so called innocent daughter,
Has been looking at the Nepalese with lustful eyes.

"Shameless girl!"

This remark shocked the emperor.
He said only this much—
"Darling, don't be so suspicious."

But she continued—
"I have also heard that,
She wished to become a Tara, too—
Like White Tara or Green Tara.

"Ugh! Looks so tender.
But, so brazen in deeds!"

Having said so, she left in anger.

He tried, but could not stop her.

Her maids followed her.
The maids assisting the emperor also nervously followed her.

xxx

Like a statue the emperor remained,
Down the stage nearby a stone lion.

Miao Yen arrived there in tears.
Two young maids that followed are wiping her tears.

The emperor asked—
"Something wrong?"

Sighing, she poured her resentments—

"On the hallway,
Beautiful mom stared at me with crooked eyes.

"Murmured— 'Tara or Randy, I will see!'"

xxx

Miao Yen's tears made the emperor very sad.
Amidst mounting tension, he said to himself—
"How I happened to pick up this nasty woman,
As my dearest love-partner!

"What a headache!

"No doubt, this girl is her stepchild.
But, she should have become an ideal stepmother,
Loving and caring than a true mother.

"On the contrary,
This woman turned up always jealous,
Always trying to find out faults!"

Moments later,
Miao Yen spoke, wiping her tears—
"Papa,
I mentioned about the Dagoba to be built.
And, Teacher Lao told me the story on Sweta Aswo Mahavihar.
He said, Sweta means white and white has much significance."

The emperor was relieved to see his daughter talking.
He asked—
"What else did he say?"

She told what she was told—
"Emperor Ming of Han Dynasty had a dream, one night.
He saw Sakyamuni.
The next day, consulting with his ministers,
He dispatched a group in search of manuscripts.

"Pragyaparmita and other manuscripts on Buddhism,
Were carried to Chang An on the back of a white horse.
Then, the first ever monastery was built there.
It was named Sweta Aswo Mahavihar."

Having listened this,
The emperor's mind flew to Sweta Aswo Mahavihar.

Miao Yen added quickly—
"Papa, take me too with you when you go to Chang An."

While the conversation was going on like this,
A senior messenger came and reported—
"Your Majesty!
The commander-in-chief is coming to see you."

The emperor was choked.
He ordered— "Tell him to come."

He thought—
"Could it be that,
Somewhere someone is trying to create trouble?"

He, again, talked with his daughter—
"So, the fact that,
The Dagoba to be built is to be named 'White Dagoba',
Seems quite appropriate.

"Am I right?"

Having said 'Right',
She tried to compare Sweta Aswo Mahavihar,
That she has never visited,
With the White Dagoba, sketched recently in a piece of paper.

Soon, a tall warlord came.
The deputy warlord followed.

The tall warlord reported—
"Your Majesty,
I came here with strange news."

He continued—
"With Your Majesty's great efforts,
Yuan Dynasty has been well established.
Mongol, Han, or Ugur;
Chang, Chui or Kwai;
Whatever be the race,
All have become united as one.
The main gate of the central Yangtse River,
And Siang Giang,
Is about to fall into our hands.

"At a time like this,
Already crippled mad jackals—Chiang and Kwai—,
Are once again trying to raise their heads."

Mention of these names made the emperor mad.
Furious, he looked as if he was charging in a battlefield.
Seemingly, he was roaring on the back of a neighing horse—
Reins in the left hand and sword in the right hand.

He commanded—
"Go!
Net them like fishes!
Skin their backs!
If they don't yield, cut off their heads!

"Go, don't delay!
Or, should I go myself?
I myself shall kill them.
You know, I am the grandson of Thai Su.
I have already destroyed many enemies like them.

"This Yuan Dynasty of mine!
I have sweated blood over this empire.
I won't let anyone to encroach on its identity."

Nervous at the sight of this terribly furious emperor,
The tall warlord spoke softly—
"Your Majesty, we are still alive.
We are not dead.
We will carry out your order.
We shall capture them.
And kill them if necessary.
Please excuse us, we are moving now."

Quickly, they moved.

Horrified,
Miao Yen is silently feeling,
The untold sorrows and sufferings,
Of thousands of wounded war victims.

Trees and plants have begun to sprout.
Birds are trilling, chirping or cooing.
Warm sunshine is trying to wake up sleeping ponds and rivers.
Once again, New Year has begun with the spring season.

All over the country,
People are celebrating Chun-jie festival.

Cheerful voices in each house reflected—
Everybody is in festive mood irrespective of rich or poor.

xxx

The palace is specially decorated.

Big porcelain pots are placed in orderly manner.
Chinese lanterns and large portraits of the emperor are hung.
Flags, pennants, buntings and banners are fluttering in the wind.

Magnificent throne with dragons is well set on the dais.
Displayed close to the throne are some covered objects.

Nearby, Pasapa and Arniko are conversing in whispers.

xxx

The emperor arrived.

Everybody greeted him in one voice,
On the occasion of the New Year Spring Festival.

Cheerfully accepting the greetings,
The emperor sat into the throne.

Among the accompanying royal ladies,
Miao Yen's presence excelled the others'.
She looked marvelous in her new-year-dress.

The emperor began to talk—
"Teacher, when did you come back from Than Cha Sa?
Are you fine?"

Pasapa answered—
"Just yesterday.
By grace of Your Majesty, everything is fine."

Miao Yen picked up the words 'Than Cha Sa'.

She queried—
"Papa, how far is Than Cha Sa from here?"

The emperor smiled and replied—
"Your questions shall be answered by the Teacher.
You just listen to him."

Obligated, Pasapa began—
"Two days at quick pace,
Otherwise three days from here.

"Must cross three ridges of forest hills,
Then follow long zigzag trails.
Between the hills,
Nearby a rivulet in the middle of the forest,
Lies Than Cha Sa.

"The trails of smoke coming out of incense sticks,
Offered by monks and nuns,

"To Sakyamuni in the big monastery there,
Are seen ever rising up above the pine trees.

"It is an immortal creation of Shin Dynasty Emperors.
It is a place for those who want to remain in meditation.
The glories of Than Cha Sa can't be described in words."

Naturally, Miao Yen's eager mind flew towards Than Cha Sa.

Moments later, at the indication of Pasapa,
Arniko uncovered the covered objects one by one.

He looked towards the emperor and spoke—
"Your Majesty,
On the happy occasion of Chun-jie,
I am offering these images to Your Majesty."

As the three images came into view,
The beauty of the hall became even more colorful.

And, a big round of applause followed.

Fascinated,
The emperor appreciated Arniko with these words—
"Nepalese gentleman,
Great are your skilled hands."

Miao Yen stepped towards the images,
And looked at them with keen interest.

In fact, all the eyes of those who were present there,
Were focused on these gilded images.

xxx

This time, the emperor opened his heart—
"Teacher,
These days I have no peace.
I don't know why!
Physically, I am not a sick person."

Pasapa understood the secrets of the emperor.
He said—
"Your Majesty,
Material achievements of any kind—
The throne, the beloved ones, people or prosperity etc.—
Can't give enduring peace.

"To have peace of mind,
We should be able to meet the Pragya in the inside of us.

"In the beginning,
Sakyamuni, too, was a victim of anxiety as we are now.
He understood the truth and met with Pragya inside him.
Meditating underneath Bodhi Tree, he attained Bodhigyan.
Only then he became Buddha.

"But, it is not possible to meet Pragya till the mind is shadowed.
The illness of mind needs some medicine.
And that medicine is Dharma.

"Individuals following Buddha and Dharma constitute Sangha.
Buddha, Dharma and Sangha together is regarded Tri Ratna.
Today is the New Year day and first day of spring season.
Let us pray for World Peace on this special occasion."

The emperor was relieved for the time being.
He was impressed by the words—
Buddha, Dharma and Sangha.

xxx

As the evening approached,
Smart young maids with rosy cheeks strode the hallway.
They chatted and patted while putting oil-lamps on the doors.

Meanwhile,
Two buffoons wearing masks came towards the hall.

They bowed and announced—
"Your Majesty!
We have message from Empress Wang Chung—
'It's time to stage the drama'."

The very spell of 'drama' filled the hall with excitement.
The emperor headed towards the balcony facing the courtyard.

The people gathered in the courtyard greeted him in one voice—
"Long live the Emperor!
Happy New Year and Happy Spring Festival to Your Majesty!"

Cheerful emperor responded warmly—
"You can start now!"

xxx

The great monk Huang Tsang slowly appeared on the stage,
Chanting prayers of Avlokiteswar.
He is making a pilgrimage towards the Land of Buddha.

He is followed by Sun Woo Kung,
Who somersaulted in progression.

Fa Kwa and Fi Kwa also appeared in humorous movements.

The audience cheered at the sight of these actors.
But, some children nervously crept towards their parents.

xxx

The drama with music is going on in a grand manner.

The audience is so much absorbed in the drama,
They felt, they too were going on in this pilgrimage.

But, Arniko's mind is in Nepal.
He reckoned that in next five days,
Nepal would be observing Sri Panchami.

He remembered,
The celebration of Spring Ceremony on the Manjeswari Hill.

The folk song of the season resounded into his ears—
'On the green tree, the yellow bird has once again come to sing.'

xxx

The emperor left after the program ended.
The audience started dispersing.
But, Miao Yen stepped towards the dais once again.

She gently touched the images.
The more she looked at them, the more attractive they looked.

Moments later, she unconsciously ventilated her feelings—

"Do you know?

I am told,

The Nepalese gentleman belongs to a family of Sakyabansa.

"And, my papa says,

He may be closely related to Sakyamuni,

Who previously was a prince."

But,

Her maids could not understand what she wanted to point out.

They just looked at each other and nodded.

Seated on the highest spot of the Great Wall,
Above the Pa Ta Ling village,
Arniko looked all around him, completely lost to the world.

One moment,
He saw the long and twisty Great Wall
As a serpent of tremendous size—
Creeping stealthily.

Next moment,
Bearing cold wind, he thought—
"Founded hundreds of years ago,
This Great Wall—
Fifteen Hand's high and fifteen Hand's wide
(Wide enough for five race-tracks)—
Is said to have become five thousand Kwe long.
It is very unique and marvelous."

He then made up his mind—
"If a huge and tall Dagoba,
Compatible with this Great Wall, can be built,
That will be a wonderful matching."

He visualized the Stupas of Swayembhu and Khasti in Nepal.
He felt proud of them,
And became encouraged and confident.

He decided—
"Rather than building a medium-size Stupa,
In three or four years' time,
The best will be, (though it may take nine or ten years),
To build the one nowhere else found in the whole world.

"That will be—
Unique in shape, size and style;
Huge and tall almost as the sky;
Vastly white in color;
Extraordinarily nice in appearance;
And, full of pious qualities.

"I will talk about this with the Emperor."

xxx

Stone built cottage, two trees on either side.
Nearby two cages— one for pigs, the other for chickens.
Moonbeams of the crescent moon dimly lit the lawn.

Food items are put as offerings in front of—
The God of the House,
The God of the Door,
And the God of the Kitchen.

The room is decorated in traditional manner.
Portraits of ancestors are hung on the walls.
Incense sticks are burnt.

The group leader introduced Arniko to the old couple—
"This gentleman is from Nepal."

The old woman remarked in astonishment—
"Oh! I took him as our own native fellow."

xxx

The guests are duly seated.

The old woman brought some wine glasses,
And a wine pot of porcelain make.
A plate of roast duck was also brought.

Pouring sparkling wine for the guests,
The old woman looked towards his old man,
And spoke sadly—
"This gentleman from Nepal resembles our son Si Chung.

"Dazed and lured to follow the cruel warlords,
This child never came back ever since he left.

"No idea, still alive or not!
His wife, gone to pay a visit to her parents,
Is also said to have gone to another man along with her baby."

The old man unconsciously sighed,
As he remembered his only son.

Deeply moved by this pathetic circumstance,
Arniko said to himself—
"I too have my parents.
I also have my wife married at early age.
What could have they thought?"

xxx

The guests, back from their trip to the Great Wall,
Are enjoying the refreshment.

The old man has something in his mind.
He filled his pipe with tobacco out of a small tobacco bag.
Then, he smoked and said—

"Gentleman from Nepal,
Do kings in Nepal also go into frequent confrontations?
And engage in battles?"

Arniko answered politely—
"I tell you something I was told by my mama.

"When I was a small child,
During the reign of King Avaye Malla,
King Mukunda Sen of Palpa,
That lies west of Nepal Valley,
Intruded into the valley.

"The limitless atrocities and killings by this king,
Enraged Pasupatinath, the God of Nepal.
The Nepalese people chased him.
He died on the way a painful and sorrowful death."

The old man nodded and said—
"The god in your country is so sensible and so powerful."

The old woman said refilling the wine glasses—
"Nepalese gentleman,
This country of ours is a war-torn country.

"The Great Wall you just visited is also,
Built for strategic purpose.

"This massive stone-work is filled with,
Sweated labor of peoples of many generations."

She went on opening her sorrowful heart—

"Now that we are already old, our life is very short.
When the death comes, we can't resist.
So, we are losing our hope to die in peace.
How can we smile in a situation like this?"

Arniko thought of Tri Bodhi Chita for a while.
Then he told this old couple,
Something about Tri Bodhi Chita in brief.

"When the mind is shadowed by ignorance,
It will always cry.
It can smile only when it is illuminated by Pragya.

"If we learn to observe the Charya of creating Tri Bodhi Chita,
By reciting prayers,
It will always do well."

Interested, the old woman moved closer and said—
"Nepalese gentleman,
We got something beyond our expectation.
Please don't go without having told us,
About this Charya in detail."

The old man supported his wife—
"Nepalese gentleman,
For us,
Your coming here today is like the coming of angels."

The other members in the group commented—
"This is something we should learn too."

Arniko concentrated for a while.
Then, he began to speak—

"First of all, say Namaskar to Tri Ratna.

"Then, create Bodhi Pranidhi Chita,
By taking a vow of doing good deeds.

"Then, create Bodhi Prasthan Chita,
By observing Charya of doing good deeds.

"Then, create Bodhi Parinamana Chita,
To offer Punya to Bodhi.

"To be able to get rid of all the worldly desire,
Is to attain Nirvana.
Be resolute to attain this Nirvana!

"Surrender this Nirvana thus attained, too,
To that very same Bodhi,
For the betterment of all the living beings.

"If we learn to observe this Charya,
Even if Yemraj comes to take us,
He will give us honor and take us to the heaven."

xxx

The old couple,
Listening attentively to Arniko,
Seemed to have experienced a carefree world, momentarily.

Seeing them like this, Arniko thought—
"No doubt, this couple is cultured with pious background.
Just a polishing touch has led them to concentration."

When inquiry was made about their surname, by the way,
All the facts became clear.
They were of Chou origin.

When Monk Thau An established,
The first ever Buddhist Association,
They became the members.
Since then, their surnames were converted to Si.

Later, it was revealed that,
The two words, 'Si' of China and 'Sakya' of Nepal,
Have the same significance.

xxx

All of a sudden,
The long talk was interrupted.

A woman from the neighborhood came crying—
"Help! Help!!"

They asked in one voice—
"What's the matter?"

She said—
"Two Mongols on horseback,
Kidnapped my young daughter, just now."

Carrying torches in their hands,
And shouting— "Stop! … Stop!! …",
They went out running in search and rescue.

The full moon becomes smaller and smaller,
And vanishes.

The new moon grows bigger and bigger,
And turns into full moon.

In fact, the size of the moon neither decreases nor increases.
It is always one, always full.

However in practice,
There is a tradition,
To begin new projects at suitable moments on suitable days.

Such suitable days and moments are selected,
With respect to different phases of the moon.

Following this tradition, Arniko decided that—
The date of laying foundation stones should be,
The slowly approaching full moon day.

xxx

A big welcome-gate is erected south of the construction site,
In the open field surrounded by settlements near Chin Sui River,
That flows east of Fu Che Men gate in a long serpentine course.

Beside the images of lions on either side of this welcome-gate,
Two jars filled with clean holy water are placed.

Fastened overhead are the banners,
That read Buddha, Dharma and Sangha.

White, yellow, blue, red and green colored buntings,
Representing Pancharasmi, are also fastened all around.

Sweet smelling smoke is rising up above the big censers,
Filled with frankincense.

Sweet smell is also coming,
Out of the burning of the incense sticks.

xxx

The model of the White Dagoba to be built is exhibited.

Founded on Bhupur Mandala of Tantric significance,
The dome shaped middle portion looks like a huge lotus flower.

Over the dome shaped structure,
There are circular stories, representing Thirteen Heavens.

Dharma Chhatra lay over the top story.

The summit has the shape of a Purna Kalas.

xxx

A model of a monastery in Sino-Nepalese style is also exhibited.
It has five antennas like summits on the top.
And a three-in-one entrance door.

Images of Buddha and,
Lokpal, Arahat and Milapu found in Chinese monasteries,
Are also exhibited.

All of them looked very nice.

xxx

The murmur of spectators in thousands is getting noisier.

Right on time,
Emperor Hu Pi Le arrived, riding on a magnificent horse.

The empresses and princesses also arrived on sedan chairs.

Chanting prayers, Arniko welcomed the emperor.

xxx

Happy audience is cheering up amidst Mangal Dhoon.
The site, a barren land, has turned into a heavenly place.

Arniko went on briefing the emperor,
Taking reference of the exhibited models.

Pointing towards the four corners, the emperor inquired—
"What do those pennants and buntings signify?"

Arniko explained politely—
"They signify that this spot has been blessed,
By taking the Serpent God into control.

"It is necessary to do so,
In order to keep the structure firm,
As long as the sun and the moon remain in the sky."

Again, the emperor inquired—

"What about that object in the center?"

The answer was—
"Your Majesty, that is Purna Kalas, seeded with jewels.
Nava Ratna sent from the palace are put inside it."

Cheerful emperor leaped down from the horse.
Two attendants, on either side, took the horse to the other side.
Arniko escorted the emperor to the center of the spot.

For betterment of the whole world,
He urged the emperor,
"Your Majesty,
Please be ready for the rituals."

xxx

Referring Thiasafu,
And ringing chanting bell in his left hand,
Arniko chanted Sthiro Wakya prayer.

Following the gestures from Arniko,
And concentrating his mind on Bodhi Chita,
The emperor covered the Purna Kalas,
By laying five foundation stones.

Next,
Emperor Hu Pi Le proudly addressed—
"Today, in this country,
Arniko, a gentleman from Nepal,
Is engaged in building,
A unique and historic Dagoba.

"I urge each and everyone,
To extend maximum co-operation in this noble task.

"Let this White Dagoba radiate sunshine forever,
In the form of Tri Ratna,
And purify every soul!

"Let this White Dagoba remain firm,
To give beauty to this capital city of ours,
And to protect it forever!

"Let this White Dagoba keep on giving,
The message of International Brotherhood!

"Let this White Dagoba hoist and flutter,
The religious flag of Buddhism forever,
For the welfare of all the living beings!"

The sky thundered with cheers of crowds.

Later, the emperor went around the spot.
He asked—
"How high will it go?"

Arniko answered—
"Excluding the foundation,
It will be 108 Hand's high above the ground."

xxx

The emperor shared his feelings with the minister by his side—
"Certainly,
When complete,

44

"Everybody will be able to see this White Dagoba,
Touching the sky.
It will be a symbol of Friendship and World Peace."

The minister commented—
"Your Majesty,
One day,
Your farsighted vision shall be appreciated all over the world."

Delighted by the fascinating words of the minister,
The emperor rode the magnificent horse and left.

The imperial ladies also left except Miao Yen.
She stood mesmerized.

She asked someone to tell Arniko,
(Returning from the welcome-gate after seeing off the emperor),
To go towards her.

She did manage to ask—
"Gentleman,
Could you please tell me,
When will this White Dagoba be complete?"

Arniko was slightly nervous for a moment.
Next moment he controlled himself and replied courteously—
"My target is five years.
However,
Since ponds and lakes happen to freeze here in winter,
It may take seven or eight years.

"But the abundance of helping hands here,
Makes me hopeful."

Miao Yen nodded.

She could not express lot of things accumulated inside her.

Because her sedan-carriers looked impatient, she left.

xxx

Meanwhile,

An old man approached stroking his goatee and said—

"Gentleman,

You came from such a distant place like Nepal,

To build this Dagoba.

"Being old,

I personally can't give any reliable support.

But, I am sending my son for your help.

"This child, too, is very much inclined towards sculpture.

Has some skills too.

"It is my hope that—

You will take charge of this child as your disciple;

Educate him with Buddha's religious teachings;

And train him with all the skills."

Arniko asked— "What's the name of this brother?"

The answer was— "Liu Yuan."

Liu Yuan bowed three times.

Arniko saw hidden talents in his face.

He assured the old man—

"Uncle,
I shall certainly transfer,
All my knowledge and skills to this brother."

The old man felt free like a bird.
He visualized Pancharasmi rays,
Radiating out from the spot,
Where the foundation stones were laid.

Suddenly,
Up there in the sky near the eastern corner,
He saw a Door of Heaven magnificent with multi-colored rays,
Opening up!

From the other corner,
Flowers were raining down,
Gently!

Time advances at its own pace.

The moon waxes and wanes each month.

Likewise, summer after winter,
And, winter after summer passes in rotation.

However, a man fully absorbed in work,
May not be aware of the passing away of time.

The same thing happened to Arniko,
Engaged heart and soul,
In the construction of the White Dagoba.

xxx

One day,
Arniko, with tools in his hand,
Is demonstrating Liu Yuan,
To shape the image of Sakyamuni.

Looking at the sweating face of his teacher,
The disciple interrupted—
"Teacher,
I am undergoing training here,
For more than a year.
But, I never noticed your birthday."

This remark made Arniko realize that,
So much of time had passed without any notice.

He counted his fingers, sighed and said—

"Liu, it has been twelve years since I left home.
This year should be the twelve-year-anniversary,
Of chariot pulling festival of Bungadyo."

The disciple could not understand more than half,
Of what his teacher told him.
So, he looked at Arniko's face,
Anticipating he would explain more.

Arniko added—
"Liu, note it.
Bungadyo is one of the names given to Avlokiteswar.
Here, you call him Kwan Yin.

"In our country, he is also called Karunamaya or Loknath.
There, he is boarded on a huge and tall chariot.
That then is pulled around the city,
By hundreds of men from among the celebrating crowd.

"There are two temples for Bungadyo—
One in Yela and the other in Bunga.
Last time, I told you about Buddha, Dharma and Sangha.
Yes, the leading figure of this Sangha,
Is none other than Avalokiteswar."

The disciple's interest was,
To learn more and more skills.
He gently rubbed his right hand against his head,
And put forward this question—
"Teacher,
Is it very difficult to make the image of Avalokiteswar?"

Arniko answered smilingly—

"Liu, I understand the idea behind your question.
You just be prepared to take.
I will systematically transfer to you,
All my knowledge and all my skills,
One by one, in due course of time."

While the conversation was going on like this,
Wang Ming the head manual worker came and said—
"Sir, a group of visitors wants to meet you.
They look important persons.
But I don't know what they are really after."

Arniko commented—
"Perhaps, they have come to win a contract to supply stones."

Later, it became clear that they had come for something else.
After seating them in his workplace, Arniko spoke softly—
"I suppose, you came from quite afar.
Please let me know, if I am of any service to you."

The visitors were impressed,
By the gracious manners of Arniko— a charming young man.

As Liu began filling porcelain cups with black tea,
The leader of the group began to talk—
"Nepalese gentleman,
We are from Kiang Si Province.
Actually we came to this city,
To call on Emperor Hu Pi Le on official matters.

"He talked about the White Dagoba under construction,
And strongly advised us to pay a visit here.
And, also to meet you.

"We were informed that you are in the workplace.
So we came right over here to meet you."

Next, the secretary in the group informed,
About the man who just spoke—
"Nepalese gentleman,
He is Chiang Sung Lai, our Teacher.
In fact, he is an Incarnation of Taoism."

Arniko bowed down towards Chiang Sung Lai.
In no time, he managed to make a seat higher than other seats.
In spite of the words 'No, that's not necessary!' repeatedly,
Arniko humbly persuaded him to sit on this special seat.

Broad minded Arniko,
Taking an opportunity to learn something new,
Expressed—
"I often hear about Taoism.
Today, by chance, you happened to come right over here.
I would like to hear something about Taoism from you."

His Holiness concentrated for a moment,
Memorized Hermit Lao Che and explained—
"Tao is hidden inside Samyak doctrine.
Birth and death are just the turns of a life cycle.
Everything we see in this world is perishable.
If there is anything everlasting, that is Tao.

"Tao is imperishable and eternal.
When the mind is free from desire or ambitions,
Tao is attained.

"We may talk about Taoism endlessly.

"But what I told, in brief, are the rudiments of Taoism.

"By the way,
We are also interested,
To learn something about Sakyamuni from you."

Arniko prayed Tri Ratna for a moment.
Then he began to speak—
"Actually, I am just a son of an artisan.
But, I dare to tell you something,
That I heard from my parents and teachers.

"Sakyamuni discovered the Four Truths—
Human beings have misery;
Misery has cause;
Extinction of misery is practicable;
There is a way for extinction of misery.

"Knowledge of Four Truths leads to Nirvana.
Nirvana itself is an illusory belief.
It is Pratityasamutpad as well as,
Nothingness or emptiness or illusoriness.

"In other words,
Nothing or no religion in this world,
Has a free quality or free existence.
Everything is but the nothingness,
Like the emptiness of the sky.

"However, when covered by grey clouds,
Because of limited knowledge and illusions,
It is said that the sky is cloudy, dark, gloomy, etc.

"Even imaginary pictures of various shapes and sizes,
Are seen in the sky.

"If we see the sky through the eyes of Pragya,
We realize that the sky has never changed.
It is neither gloomy nor dark nor bright.
In reality, it is without any self-existence."

Next, Arniko led the group to the construction site.
He briefed them,
About the plan and progress of the construction work.

One of them raised this question—
"What is the true significance of a Dagoba?"

Arniko explained—
"Once again, I am only a son of an artisan.
I have my own view points.
For me,
What Sakyamuni had told is religious science as well as an art.
That's why, Buddhism is always supported by art and culture.

"In this context,
This Dagoba under construction,
Is a spiritual embodiment of awakened mind.
In other words,
It is Swayembhu or Prabhaswar or emptiness.

"Salt dissolved in water is not visible.
Likewise, ghee in milk is also not visible.
But, after some processing,
We can take out lumps of salt from its solution in water.
And, ghee from milk.

"Similarly, this White Dagoba is a medium,
To convert Chita into Bodhi Chita,
In the process of attaining Bodhipad.

"There are many significance of a Dagoba.
They can't be told in words."

Tao Guru remarked gladly—
"What you told us seems very important.
During our journey,
On the way,
We have seen many artifacts.

"We wondered why pains had been taken for years and years,
To build so many of them.

"Now we understood the truth behind them.
The masterpieces like—
Tung Hwang in Kansu;
Long Men in Hanan;
Yung An in Sansi;
And the excellent artifacts,
On the foothills of Da Chu Mountains in Sa Chwan!
All of them constitute,
The practical medium of learning Buddhism."

Arniko said politely—
"That's right! That's right!!"

Tao Guru further said—
"Let me tell you something that I have been told.
It was five hundred years ago,
During the reign of Tang Dynasty.

"Chen Chan,
The chief monk of Yang Che Wo Buddhist Monastery,
Was requested and persuaded by some Japanese scholars,
To go with them to their country.
As a result, Buddhism flourished in Japan too."

Listening this,
Arniko's mind became eager to fly south,
Cross the China Sea and reach Japan in the east.
And see this country personally.

Tao Guru changed the topics.
He began to say—
"We are planning to build a huge Tao temple,
In the mountains called,
The Flying Serpent and the Flying Tiger.

"We will put an image of Hermit Lao Che inside this temple.
We need your help and honest advice on this matter."

Arniko responded warmly—
"Certainly, I will do what I can.
But, one thing,
While making the image of Lao Che with these hands of mine,
Often used to make Sakyamuni's images,
There is a chance—
Lao Che's face may look slightly like the face of Buddha."

Tao Guru smiled and said—
"That doesn't matter."

xxx

The visitors were seen off.
Arniko came back with Liu to his workplace.
He expressed his feelings—
"This country China has a vast chest."

Puzzled Liu said—
"Teacher, I couldn't understand what you said."

Arniko said—
"The heart of you Chinese People is like a lotus flower."

The disciple felt his chest putting his hand on it.
Supposing it as a lotus flower that originates in the mud,
And emerges above water without getting wet,
He used his head and realized many facts.

The White Dagoba is gradually protruding up,
Above the foundation built with Tantric procedures.

Artisans are working like ants in the four directions.

On-lookers are dreaming of the day,
When they might see the White Dagoba in complete form.

Pausing a while from his work,
Arniko headed towards his workplace.

He drank some water and lay down to take rest.
At this very moment,
There came a messenger from the imperial palace,
And handed him a letter.

Guessing it a letter from his home after a long time,
He rose up quickly and opened it.
Just then, Liu arrived there on a tea break.

Noticing the letter being read,
He could not resist asking—
"Teacher, a letter from Nepal.
Am I right?"

Arniko answered without removing his eyes from the letter—
"It's from Lhasa.
Teacher Pasapa wrote about the renovation work,
In the Potala Durbar Square.
He did mention some news from Nepal too."

Impatient, the disciple asked quickly—
"Teacher, may I know the news from Nepal?"

Arniko replied, showing the letter—
"Oh, yes."

He added—
"It is the matter of time.
Nobody can stop it.
Days of King Jayasingh Malla have come to an end.
Ananta Malla is the new king now.

"He is said to be liberal and religious minded.
It is mentioned that,
He has engaged Buddhist scholars in every monastery,
To prepare manuscripts on Pragyaparmita.

"Next,
It is mentioned that,
Chakreswar, the chief of Saka Baha in Yela,
Has sent a letter to Hyese of Sa Sakya Monastery in Lhasa,
With a proposal to establish friendly ties.

"Along with the letter,
An illuminated manuscript on Astasahastrika Pragyaparmita,
Has been sent as gift.
It is in the ink of gold and packed inside a gilded silver box."

Pra-gya-pa-ra-mi-ta resounded in the ears of the disciple,
Who is never tired of making inquiries.
He asked— "Teacher, what is Pragyaparmita?"

Holding the letter in his hand and closing his eyes,
Arniko concentrated on Pragyaparmita for a while.
Then reciting Hridayasutra, he opened his eyes and said—

"Listen Liu.
I am trying to answer your question as I can,
With my limited knowledge.

"The middle path discovered by Sakyamuni,
Derived a liberal type of doctrine,
Known as Madhyamik Darsan.

"Nagarjun and other scholars had heavily taxed their brains,
To nourish this doctrine.
That resulted in the development of a separate philosophy,
Known as Pragyaparmita."

Still interested, Liu expressed what he felt—
"Teacher,
You are a teacher, not only on arts,
But also on religion.
I wonder how I can grasp this Pragyaparmita."

Conversation was going on like this.
Curious workers began to gather in.
Consequently,
The workplace turned into a small hermitage,
Similar to Gridhakut.

Arniko recited Charya prayers on Pragyaparmita,
And talked about Panchaskandha—
"When something is imagined out of nothingness,
What comes ahead first is an appearance.
It has— name, smell, taste, touch-ability and religion.

"Naturally,
The eyes to see the appearance;

"The ears to hear the name;
The nose to smell;
The tongue to taste;
The body to touch;
And, the mind to follow the religion becomes necessary.

"The appearance comes into existence,
Only when it is being imagined.

"In other words,
Imagination is the source of every desire or anxiety or pain.

"Panchaskandha should be understood like this too—
Everything is empty by nature.
They are without any self-existence or appearance.
They are like the vast sky which is appearance-less."

Liu gave a quick and serious thought on what Arniko said.
The others also tried to understand.
But Liu was the sharpest among them.

He asked—
"Teacher, just last night I saw one panda in my dream.
It was fat, and, black and white in color.
One moment it was chewing bamboo leaves.
Next moment it disappeared and was lost within the dream.
Is this related to Panchaskandha, too?"

Arniko replied with a smile—
"Yes.
The panda you saw in your dream has emerged out of nothing.
It was a panda with appearance.
It was an appearance-less panda, too, lost into emptiness.

"Don't forget,
Appearance is not separate from emptiness.
Nor emptiness is separate from appearance.
They are relative things.
This is what one should understand."

Liu asked again—
"Teacher,
I have been told by my father that,
Such type of creatures are often encountered,
While passing through the forests in Santung Province.

"They are the real pandas seen in daytime, not in dream.
What you call them?
I don't understand this."

Arniko concentrated a moment, then explained—
"Liu,
In the final analysis,
Those real pandas with appearance,
Are also nothing but emptiness."

Liu and other persons present there reacted in one voice—
"How can the pandas,
Clearly seen in front of us in reality,
Be nothing but emptiness?
This is very strange."

Arniko reached for a lump of clay, nearby.
Quickly, he shaped a panda out of it.
And put it on the floor.

He then asked them pointing at it—

"What is that?
A lump of clay or a panda?"

"Panda!" was the answer in one voice.

He squeezed the panda,
And turned it into a lump of clay,
And asked—
"What do you say this time?"

Everybody replied in one voice—
"A lump of clay."

He smiled and said—
"What happens,
If we go on breaking up this clay,
Into infinitely small pieces?"

Nobody answered.
Everyone was thinking.

Arniko explained—
"Just emptiness or zero without any self existence.
But, this zero is not the same zero in daily counting.
It is the zero or emptiness or nothingness,
To be seen through the knowledge of Samyak Sambodhigyan.

"In fact, if we understand it clearly,
It is a state of mind,
Where all the imaginations cease,
And only nothingness remains."

Liu shook his head in confusion and commented—

"Teacher,
Those pandas I mentioned are,
Not only with appearance,
They are live too.
They can roar and climb the trees."

Arniko explained gesturing with his hands—
"Panda, be it with appearance or with life,
Go to the place from where it has originated.
Then we see that it was just a drop.

"Break up this drop into minute particles.
Then we see that this panda,
Even if it could dance,
Is nothing but something that has emerged out of zero,
And is merging back to zero.
Its appearance and its life get lost.

"Not only that panda,
We human beings are also the same."

Having said so, Arniko drank some water.
Immediately, he was overwhelmed by Nirbikalpa Samadhi.
He was breathing, but standstill like a statue.

Liu and the others, present there, thought—
"Can it be that,
The Panchaskandha so called is,
The Pragyaparmita itself?"

Four years has passed unnoticeably.

Construction work in the field nearby Phing Sa Men,
Is going on for the fifth year running.

Major work remained is the construction of,
Thirteen small stories representing Thirteen Heavens.

The final work would be,
To fix a summit,
On the top of the entire structure.

xxx

One day in Da Du,
Italian explorer Marco Polo,
Who arrived there crossing seven seas and many countries,
Was granted an audience with Emperor Hu Pi Le.

During their conversation in the imperial palace,
The emperor mentioned about Arniko,
And the White Dagoba.

He emphasized—
"It is going to be a historic masterpiece."

Hearing this from the emperor's own voice,
Marco Polo became confused and impatient.

Earlier, he was proud of,
Being the first Italian fellow to visit China.

This time, he is mortified and could not keep his head erect.

He looked very sad,
Like a monkey fallen down from a tree.

He could not sleep the whole night.
He became a fish without water.

Anyway, he decided to go and see the White Dagoba once,
And meet the architect.

Next day, he headed towards the construction site,
Together with a dignitary from the palace.

When the site came into view,
The dignitary said pointing with his finger—
"Look! That's the White Dagoba under construction."

Surprised, Marco Polo expressed—
"Oh! It's a temple in a different style.
But, I thought it would be a cathedral,
Like the one in Saint Peter's Square."

As they reached closer to the site,
The dignitary said—
"Look! That one is the architect."

Marco Polo looked at him carefully,
From top to bottom and the bottom to the top.

To his satisfaction, he discovered—
Black cap;
Black hair;
Black eyes;
Broad forehead;

Cheerful look;

Nice nose;

Nice earlobes;

Pointed chin;

Groomed moustache;

Healthy complexion;

And unique costume.

He, then, concluded that,

This man is not from Naples in Italy, at the least.

It all happened like this—

The word Nepal pronounced by the emperor,

Sounded like Naples.

And, Arniko like Alfonso.

He misunderstood—

A fellow named Alfonso from Naples of his own country,

Has been building the so called White Dagoba,

Even before his arrival.

Relieved, Marco Polo stepped forward,

And introduced himself with a smile—

"I am from Italy.

My name is Marco Polo.

May I know where you are from and your name?"

Arniko said frankly—

"Here I am called Anika.

Some call me Anika Mu.

I am from Nepal."

Marco Polo,
Even though he looked well educated and well informed,
Had so far, no idea about Nepal and its whereabouts.

He asked—
"Where is this country Nepal situated?"

Arniko explained—
"You know Tibet of the Great China.
Just south of Tibet lies Nepal.

"The great Himalayas,
Resided by Lord Shiva and Goddess Parvati,
Lie in northern Nepal.

"Dense forest of Kapilvastu,
Nearby Lumbini the birth-place of Lord Buddha,
Lies in southern Nepal."

Listening this,
Marco Polo's sharp mind discovered,
Many mysterious facts about Nepal.

He picked up his feather-pen and noted down,
The facts about Nepal in his notebook.

xxx

Afterwards,
Having inspected the construction site to their satisfaction,
They got seated.

Marco Polo had a query—

"Mr. Arniko,
What is the idea,
Behind the construction of this White Dagoba?"

While Arniko got himself prepared to answer this question,
Spectators began to crowd in.

Liu was eagerly watching how his teacher would answer.

Arniko recited a prayer,
From Ye Dharma Hetu Prabhava in lyrical voice.
Then he began to speak—
"You know,
In this world of ours,
Whatever we see,
Each of them has a separate cause for its existence.

"Birth, aging and death are all because of some cause.

"Pain or anxiety has its cause too.

"To root out the cause of the pain,
We must convert our Chita into Bodhi Chita.

"This Dagoba will be a spiritual and symbolic medium,
To convert Chita into Bodhi Chita."

Marco Polo shook his head and commented—
"Mr. Arniko, this White Dagoba is perishable.
To think,
It will convert Chita into Bodhi Chita,
May perhaps be only delusion.
I don't know."

This comment confused Arniko a bit.
He thought for a moment.
Then, he approached for his favorite fife,
That he used to play whenever he was in mood.

He said holding his fife—
"Mr. Marco Polo,
Isn't this fife a perishable thing?"

Marco Polo answered—
"Yes."

All rounder Arniko then played the fife.

It was the tune of a popular religious song,
Regarding the pray to Swayembhu Stupa,
By Manjushree Bodhisatwa.

Marco Polo could not pick up even a single word in the tune.
But, slowly, he was completely absorbed in it.
He came back to himself, only after Arniko started to speak.

"Mr. Marco Polo,
Of course this fife is perishable.
Still, it is the cause of the music we just listened to.

"However, we must have adequate practice,
To produce music out of it.

"Again, this fife is just an instrument,
Or medium or means, not the end.

"This White Dagoba is also a medium.

"One who masters the practice of Charya,
Entwined with a Dagoba,
Shall go on converting one's Chita into Bodhi Chita.

"This is something to be experienced and learned oneself.
I think I have made the points clear."

Marco Polo shook his head in negative gesture.

Arniko said—
"Please look!
This White Dagoba has a real appearance.

"But, if we go on taking out stone-bricks and cement,
And demolish it,
This appearance will disappear.

"The ability to perceive the disappearance of real things,
Leads to the attainment of the knowledge on nothingness."

He fished into his pocket and took out a grain of paddy.
Saying, "Let me give you another example",
He put it on his palm and explained—
"Surely, there is rice inside this paddy.
But we hardly give a thought on the constituents of rice.
No doubt, there is a drop inside it that grows rice plant.

"If we go on searching the drop inside the drop,
That would be infinitely small like the molecules and atoms.
This infinitely small drop grows rice plant that bears paddy.

"The plant dies, but the paddy becomes seed,
That reproduces paddy.

"We may see this grain of paddy from different angles as—
Appearance, pain, name, culture, and science.

"To know what this paddy grain is to know oneself by the one,
And to know the omnipresent Bodhigyan.

"So, I repeat—
This White Dagoba is an easy means to acquire Bodhigyan."

Marco Polo nodded, smiled and said—
"Well, Mr. Arniko,
Now, I understood something. Thanks."

He shook hands with Arniko and left.
On the way, he shared his feelings with the dignitary—
"Three things impressed me in this country.
The Da Du Durbar Square,
The Stone Bridge,
And, the White Dagoba.

"This Da Du metropolis is built in a well planned manner.
The wide roads all around,
Give it the look of a huge chessboard.

"The boundary walls, pillars, ponds, canals and gates,
Are like security bastions.

"The Durbar Square in the form of a platform,
Is like a heaven on the earth.

"Next, the Lu Kou Chew stone bridge,
With more than four hundred and fifty stone-lions,
In different styles!

"This is a wonderful masterpiece,
And one of the wonder of the wonders.

"And, the White Dagoba still under construction,
With the combination of art, religion and philosophy!
It is like a mirror of civilization."

Construction work of Chakrabali,
In the upper portion of the White Dagoba, is going on.

Chakrabali, symbolic of Thirteen Heavens,
Is a combination of thirteen concentric circles,
One above the other.

It looks like a magnified version of Basundhara's Sinhamu.

Whenever someone interested had queries,
About the meaning of this and that,
Arniko answered them without stopping his work.
His answers included the mention of Srawak Yan and Bajra Yan.

Those who understood,
Started the practice of reciting,
The names of Thirteen Heavens like this—
Pramudita, Bimala, Prabhakari, Archichasmati … … …

Those who didn't understand,
Tried to understand by asking further questions.

The White Dagoba is not yet complete.
But, its nearing perfection is already seen.

xxx

The day of Sa Yuan Thau has arrived once again in rotation.
The birthday of Sakyamuni is being observed,
With great enthusiasm.

Groups of Chisya's, singing hymns, are coming,
To orbit the White Dagoba under construction.

Some devotees came with pots, full of beans.
They stopped at different places around the White Dagoba,
To pray 'Namo Amitabha' and to offer the beans.

Some well-to-do followers of the religion,
Following the customary practice,
Are offering two handfuls of boiled beans to the workers as well.

Arniko, too,
Extended his hands,
And, received the beans as Pancha Daan,
Reciting— "Daanam Bibhusanam."

xxx

One night in the imperial palace,
Pillow talk is going on.

She said—
"Darling, think about the Nepalese gentleman.
His life is being spoilt in the construction of the White Dagoba.

"Poor lonely fellow, perhaps, thirty-five years in age!
I am afraid, all his desire and romance of life are drying up,
Too early, at the youthful age of vigor and vitality.

"Of course, you did tell me that,
You have already written to Teacher Pasapa,
Urging him to send messengers to Nepal,
To bring his wife here.

"But, I very really doubt whether she will come or will be sent.

"It is very difficult for a lady, who never crossed the Valley,
To cross the Himalayas.

"Poor girl, she must have been crying all the time.
It is truly said that male persons have no caring heart."

He quickly turned towards her,
And reacted with mixed feelings—
"Honey,
Your ideas are always loaded with typical petticoat views."

She retorted—
"Your Majesty,
No doubt, you may say that,
Once again I am putting forward petticoat views.

"But, it is not fair to talk like this and that,
And look down upon women by you males,
Born out of women wombs.

"Don't forget!
Women-wisdom has done many miracles too,
At proper places and proper times.

"Don't you remember?
Just last year,
Miss Huang Tao Po came here,
And demonstrated the new technology of weaving."

He didn't speak, but, thought seriously—
"That's right.
The new technology developed by Miss Huang Tao Po,
Will bring about great changes,

"In the socio-economic life of the people.
And, will add new chapter of civilization.

"And Arniko!
If he is kept as a lonely fellow throughout the years,
Sooner or later, he may remember his home.
And go back to his country.

"Even if he resides here and lives like a monk,
There will be no offspring from him."

Having thought so,
He comforted her, holding her hands—
"Alright Honey, now I realized.
What's your plan then?"

Flattered, she posed proudly one moment.
The next moment, she smiled.

After a short pause, she explained—
"Dear Majesty,
I have made up my mind,
To get this Nepalese gentleman wedded with a niece of mine.

"This child is quite pretty and cheerful too.
They match perfectly."

He could not comment anything, except—
"Alright, do as you wish."

At the same time,
Being unable to express the feelings inside his heart,
His vision blurred in confusion.

Spouse's mind reader, she understood his psychology.
And, said sympathetically—
"Darling, you have something in your mind.
Isn't it that someone has come with Miao Yen's proposal?
Or, that she decided to go herself away with a life-partner?"

He did not speak.

Moments later,
He was compelled to diffuse the facts loaded inside his heart—
"Yes.
Visiting gentleman Marco Polo has advised me that,
It is good to extend imperial relationship,
Beyond national boundaries.

"He also said that,
Around Persian countries,
There are families with backgrounds suitable for us."

She reacted in jealousy—
"So, this gentleman suggested, too, that,
He himself will act as a matchmaker. Right?"

The emperor said the truth— "That's the fact."

She commented—
"Your Majesty,
Don't expect you can send this aging girl—
Always shouting 'Namo Amitabha! Namo Amitabha!!'—
Away as a bride.

"If I talk, that would be too much.
But, I know all the facts about her."

This nasty comment disturbed him,
And made him to act as if he had fallen into sleep.

xxx

Days passed, months passed.

Once again,
New Year has come, along with the new spring season.

Surviving the dreadful cold,
The plum trees are flourishing with colorful blossoms.

After chanting the evening prayers,
Arniko lay on the bed, completely tired.

He saw moonbeams piercing into his dark room.

He peeped out of the window and saw the moon in the sky.

Thoughts came into his mind—
"Say moonlight or the moon, it is the same thing.
Of course, the moon in the sky is thousands of yards away.
But, when sighted, we can enclose it within our eyes."

He slept thinking this and that.
In his dream, he saw a cuckoo.
It was whispering into his ear and teasing him—
"Oh, lonely fellow! Oh, lonely fellow!!"

All of a sudden, he stood up.
Then he washed his face.
And, gradually recovered from sleepiness.

Moments later, he thought—
"To what place I belonged and where am I staying?
What, if I suddenly die,
Like the going out of a flickering oil-lamp?

"Perhaps, I shall dry up within myself,
And die without any issue."

He, then, happened to enter,
Into the world of his own imagination.

The wall in front of him served like a screen,
Upon which various pictures about his journey,
Are being projected, one after another.

First of all,
He saw the elephant-headed snow-capped mountain—
The Ganesh Himal.

He had seen it clearly from Na Kwa on the way,
During his set out from the Nepal Valley,
Where his home is situated.

Next, he saw the Silu Kunda,
That comes after crossing Sangu in the upward direction.

Next, the groups of people moving ahead, singing Silu Mye.

Next, the trails,
Where men, horses, donkeys, cows, buffaloes,
Sheep, goats and yaks travel.

Next, the rivers, hills, settlements, inns and Chautaras.

Next,

The monasteries with buntings on the hilltops;

The passes, valleys, Gadh's at snowlines;

The Kuti's, Jhikhachhen, Tingri Plains;

The shelter for sheep, goats and yaks built on snowy lands;

And the snowy hills.

Next, the chilly freezing wind.

Next,

The frightening experience,

While crossing Trisuli, Brahmaputra, Lhasakhusi,

And Yangshikhusi rivers on boats—

Rowing over high currents.

Next, the sharing of feelings by gesture with passers-by,

Who had different mother tongue,

Customs, costumes and culture.

He saw his own footsteps that started with 'zero',

And extended beyond uncountable number,

But, linked together in one series.

Further, he recollected his memories,

About learning of Tibetan language in Lhasa,

And, Mongol and Mandarin languages in other parts of China.

Had seen whatever happened,

And eaten whatever found.

This is how he survived.

In the meantime, he felt he has forgotten something.

So, he pinched himself on his chest.

Then he found him within himself.
He looked back and saw—
A Pipal tree has grown in Nepal.

It is getting taller and taller into tremendous size.

Whereas, thousands of leaves on it are dancing with the breeze,
Its shadow has covered a vast area on the ground.

xxx

The coincidence is that—
Some other day,
The imperial matchmaker came for some private talks.

His words sounded like a dream.
One moment Arniko was worried.
Next moment he was relieved.

This situation persisted for quite some time.

At last, Arniko was persuaded to give an answer.
He said—
"Any grant from the palace,
Be that a small coin, is an invaluable prize for me."

Getting this desired answer,
The imperial matchmaker thought his mission accomplished.

He gave a quick look at the towering White Dagoba,
And said hastily—
"Gentleman,
I hear words of praise from everyone for this White Dagoba."

Then he got on his horseback and was about to leave.

Suddenly, Arniko interrupted in confusion and said—
"One thing!"

He inquired—
"Why? Did you change your mind?"

Arniko said nervously—
"No. Not exactly so.
But, I don't want any kind of publicity on this matter.
So, I won't send any music band,
Or any nuptial procession,
To take the bride in a traditional manner."

The matchmaker, holding bridle in his hand, asked—
"Why?"

Arniko replied nervously—
"I don't feel like doing so.
Again, I am alone here."

The matchmaker said with a smile—
"Nepalese gentleman, I understand you.
I promise to bring the bride right over here.
So, you may feel comfortable and be at ease."

Then he raced the horse and vanished.

xxx

Arniko entered his room.
He weighed his arguments in his mental weighing machine.

Restrained and cool headed, he said cheerfully to himself—
"This new link with the Imperial Palace will never do any harm.
Rather, it will be very fruitful.

"It is told—
'Even a small Chyampati can hold up a big house.'

"So, I too, swear—
Even if I have to stay here permanently like a son-in-law,
I won't let anyone,
Even to speak against Nepal, my motherland.

"Who knows?
Sooner or later, this Emperor who easily swallowed Thufan,
May look at Nepal, lying just south of Tibet, with wicked eyes.

"Nobody can say whether someone shall be spared,
By this ferocious Lion of Yuan Dynasty,
Determined to suppress and conquer Chaosan in the north,
And Men Tian and Chiao Che in the south.

"This Emperor is still unable to give up his ferocious behavior,
Inherited from his grand father Chen Gez Khan.
Battles are still going on at different fronts."

His mind flashed back to,
What he saw with his own eyes,
And what he heard with his own ears,
In the imperial palace a few days ago,
During his latest visit there.

Conversation was going on in the Mongo Fa Thing.
A Mongol warlord was presenting his strategies—

"What can Wen Thing Siang,
The only remaining warlord of Song Dynasty,
Who is always on hide,
Do alone?

"We should never underestimate an enemy like this.
Not even in our dream!

"Because, like a seed of fire,
It may become devastating, very rapidly.

"Moreover, to this day,
We could neither catch him alive nor kill him.

"In order to catch him alive or kill him,
Our warriors fought many battles.

"But, he escaped to Fu Chian from Chian Si,
And to Kuang Tung from Fu Chian."

The emperor's fire of anger rose up,
From the underneath of his feet.
And he bit his own teeth.

At this very moment,
Prince Chang Sung suddenly stood up and vowed—
"Papa Majesty,
I will go and catch him.
And bring here alive!"

Having said so, he looked at a portrait hung on the wall.
It was the portrait of his great grandfather in a shako hat.

His face turned red with the blood boiling inside him.
And, he too, bit his own teeth.

Everyone seated in the Mongo Fa Thing,
Admired the courage shown by the prince—
"Prince Chang Sung is a worthy son of a great father."

The emperor ordered—
"Go, Chang Sung!
Manage yourself and fight yourself!
Bring him alive, here!

"I know what I shall do with it then!"

xxx

After the flashback of the scene in the imperial palace,
A second thought came into Arniko's mind—
"In one hand,
This vast empire of Yuan Dynasty is still expanding.

"In the other hand,
Emperor Hu Pi Le is farsightedly engaged,
In the construction of this White Dagoba,
With great devotion.

"However,
In order to change his heart completely,
I have to construct,
And continue to construct more and more Dagobas,
Of different shapes and sizes,
At different places—
Converting all the battlefields within his sight into peaceful lands.

"If I can do that,
Relation between China in the north and Nepal in the south,
Shall remain cordial for ever.

"Not only during the period of this Yuan Dynasty,
But also during the period of any other dynasty or system.

"Not only with Nepal, but also with any other country,
China's relation shall remain cordial."

He, again, said to himself—
"I am the owner of my own destiny.
What has to happen will certainly happen.
And I shall see what happens."

xxx

Content with his farsighted analysis,
Arniko thought of sharing his feelings with his disciple.
So, he went to see him.

Liu was busy in his workplace melting bronze,
To pour into the moulds designed to make images.

He was sweating.

At the sight of his teacher approaching towards him,
He cleared the things away and made a seat.

Arniko got seated and opened his mouth—
"Liu, do things come into your mind as well,
While working like this?"

He smiled and answered—
"Teacher,
Just yesterday,
A son of a courtier came here and asked,
If I was interested in going for an offense.

"Go on a ship via Korean waters and attack Japan!

"A chance to see places and enjoy.
A chance to earn name and fame, and win prize.

"So, this thing is persistently coming into my mind."

Arniko asked—
"What was your answer then?"

He said—
"Teacher, my answer was straight forward.
I told him that,
This hand of mine, used to hold carving tools,
Shall not hold swords."

Arniko understood.

He expressed—
"So, the rumor that,
The Emperor is sending troops to attack Japan,
Is, in fact, true."

Liu commented—
"He wants both peace and war at the same time.
Don't know why!"

Arniko said—
"Because they are entwined."

Wise Liu asked—
"How can we separate them?"

Arniko answered closing his eyes—
"By knowing oneself,
Through the practice of Charya."

The palace granted Arniko,
A cozy little cottage in Sian Yi Li block,
To start his new life,
Persuaded to lead by changing circumstances.

As he moved in into this new house on the day of Paru,
Rumor has it all over the block,
That a newcomer has moved in.

Men in small groups can be seen here and there,
Under the trees and under the roofs,
Having loose talks.

Some small-footed fat old women are boasting,
As if they are abreast of everything.

One of them said—
"You know?
This newcomer,
Engaged in the construction of the White Dagoba,
Is going to get married with a princess."

Hands in her stomach and with irresistible laugh,
An old baby-sitter woman opened her toothless mouth—
"Then this Nepalese fellow is going to be a son-in-law,
Of we Chinese people."

This remark made the whole group to laugh belly laugh,
For quite some time.

Children at play catching crickets here and there,
Were astonished why all of them are laughing!

Next moment,
They started mimicking their laugh.

xxx

Nice little cottage roofed with corrugated tiles.
A common yard in the center.
A tall walnut tree at one corner.

Stone lions on either side of the entrance door.
Lotus flowers and birds painted,
On the upper portion of the door.

Two neighbors—
One in the east,
The other in the west.

The sunny south-facing room is Arniko's living room.
The store-room and the kitchen are towards the north.

The entrance door is decorated traditionally,
With monograms reading Double Happiness,
Symbolic of marriage ceremony-in-progress.

xxx

In the late evening,
Groups of men, carrying lanterns in their hands,
Came reeling up the street.

Men carrying dowries,
Are also turning up dripping with sweat.

Behind them came into sight a special palanquin.

Two bridesmaids,
On either side of the bride inside the palanquin,
Are telling the bride,
Not to weep,
And that they have come very near to the bridegroom's house.

As the palanquin approached near the entrance gate,
Nicely dressed matchmaker appeared on his horseback.

Whole heartedly engaged day after day,
In the construction of the White Dagoba,
Arniko is lying down on his bed, facing upwards.

He thought—
"Oh! I am going to get imprisoned inside the world of romance.
What to do now?"
And, watched the ceiling timbers— dancing!

At this very moment, Liu came and reported—
"Teacher, the imperial matchmaker has come.
The bride also arrived."

With a body full of romantic itches and nervousness,
Arniko spoke—
"Liu, what should be done now?
How things are done here?
Call your friends too.
Do whatever you think is necessary."

Soon, the neighbors turned up,
To lend their helping hands.

Wrapped up in beautiful shawl,
The bowing bride moved slowly into the room,
Aided by the two bridesmaids on either side.

Behind the bride, came the smiling matchmaker.
He said—
"Gentleman,
Please extend your hands,
And receive this young bride."

xxx

Liu and his friends are extremely busy,
Treating the bridal party.

Some are dealing with the queries.
Some are trying to make space,
For dowries and the guests.

Some are pouring Lang Siang wine,
In porcelain wine glasses,
And serving refreshments with clever humorous talks.

At a time,
When the construction work of the White Dagoba,
Is at the final stage,
Unbelievably,
The wedding of a Nepalese fellow,
Concluded in the Chinese Capital—
Warmly, but without much publicity.

xxx

Half of the night is almost gone.
But, Arniko could not sleep.
He is changing position every now and then.

The young bride silently reached a dowry-case,
And took out a pillowcase (embroidered in silk thread),
With the portrait of a pair of swans—
Kissing each other and engaged in romance.

Her tender hand, with a ring on the ring-finger,
Gently pushed this pillowcase under his head.
Still he could not sleep.

Flashback of his marriage ceremony in Nepal,
Came in front of his eyes, one by one in turns.

In one picture,
His mother came,
Unto the receiving spot outside the entrance door.

She welcomed his Nepalese bride,
Handed over the keys of the house,
And performed rituals.

Then she escorted the bride inside the house.
Solemnization followed,
And the heads of the bridegroom and the bride,
Were made to touch.

Next,
The day of washing-hair;
The worship of the Living Goddess;
The religious-picnic at Ina;

The displaying of Fish, Parrots, Aintha, Joprasad,
On the face-looking-day;
And the receiving of Khensagun,
During the first formal visit to the parents-in-law.

Once again he tried to sleep, forgetting all the past events.
But, in vain.

Then, as he turned to the other side,
He saw the round face of his new wife—
A beautiful flower of love in full bloom.

And the sound of her sleep,
Echoed into his ears in a special rhythm.

He slowly got to his feet.
And rinsed his mouth, once, with water.

He burned some incense sticks,
In front of the Buddha in a niche of the wall.

And, ringing chanting bell very feebly,
Chanted Arye Namsangiti in whispering voice.

xxx

The bride,
Who came there with a hope,
To start conjugal life,
Woke up.

As she opened her eyes,
She felt as if she was in a dream.

Under the dim oil-lamp light,
She continuously kept on looking,
At the face of this Nepalese fellow,
Who already has become her husband.

Finishing the chanting,
He looked towards his new wife.

He saw in her,
The prime of sensuous love, lust and passions—
All over her body.

xxx

The next day,
Some workers at work in the construction site,
Are making small talks and little jokes.

Some laughed and some are amazed.

Some said— "Luck is the almighty."

Some are resenting—
"No wife throughout the years but no one bothers."

Some blasphemed the God of Works.

Some are explaining—
"The Nepalese gentleman is constructing this White Dagoba,
With clean heart.
So, god blessed him.
His life has become successful."

Some are unnecessarily worried.
One of them exploded in jealousy—
"He is not the only person,
Engaged in the construction of this huge White Dagoba.
But, where is our share of the prize?"

An old man is having a wishful thinking.
He did not open his mouth, but said to himself—
"It will be better to arrange,
As many Mongol girls and Han girls,
To this Nepalese gentleman as he desires.
So that—
Being imprisoned in the love affairs,
He won't be able to go back to Nepal.

"Hopefully,
Issues from him will turn out very skilled as he is.
Or, even better."

Amidst these conversations and imaginations,
Arniko arrived there at the construction site,
Holding a long masonry tool in his hand.

He looked tired.

Everyone greeted him—
"Hello Arniko, how are you?"

Smiles came into his face.
But, he was feeling a bit shy.
He had no words to respond.

One youthful worker said jokingly—

"Mr. Arniko,
You have married so quietly,
Even a sparrow in your house might not have noticed it.

"But you have to invite us for some celebration.
How about that?"

Everybody spoke in one voice—
"Toi! Toi!!"

Arniko was now compelled to speak.
He said—
"Friends,
I will arrange a dinner party to my capacity,
After three or four days."

The others jumped with joy, exclaiming—
"Haaw! Haaw!!"

In the eighth year,
Dharma Chhatra with thirty-six tinkling bells,
Was fixed above the Chakrabali.

Above the Dharma Chhatra, Ambasha was fixed.
And, above the Ambasha,
Finally, the summit of the White Dagoba was crowned.

xxx

Arniko's undertaking has become successful.
He spoke thankfully—
"Today, with each other's co-operation,
We met with success in our undertaking.

"This White Dagoba,
In the form of Prabhaswar Swayembhu Jyoti,
Is an embodiment of religious mind of all of us.

"Let all the blessings,
Resulting from the construction of this White Dagoba,
Rescue and relieve all the living beings in the world."

These words moved the whole group to pray together—
"We will follow Buddha!
We will follow Dharma!
We will follow Sangha!"

xxx

Dismantling of scaffold is in progress,
Unfastening the hitches of the ropes,
And taking out planks and bamboo.

Cleaning work is also done in the meantime.

Gradually, the White Dagoba is becoming clearly visible,
Like the moon just clear of clouds.

Some viewers moved nearer.
Some moved a bit farther.
Some watched continuously without changing position.

The more they viewed, the more thrilled they were.

xxx

One afternoon,
A middle aged worker lost control of himself,
And is left dangling from one of the rungs,
High above the ground.

He screamed— "Oh! I am dying!"

The peers who saw all this happen, shouted—
"Lao Hwa has fallen down!"

The on-lookers screamed hysterically—
"A man has fallen down from the scaffold!"

Arniko, who was assisting at some other side,
Rushed down towards the trapped worker.

Two other workers followed him.

Lao Hwa was rescued.
He was hurt, but, without cuts.

Arniko was carrying Lao Hwa piggyback.
Suddenly, his right foot had a limp.
But, he bore the pain silently.

He said in loud voice—
"Friends, be careful while you work!
It is easier to build scaffolds,
But, not that easy to dismantle them.

"Also keep in mind that—
Even Lord Buddha was encountered by evils.
So, we must be careful at all the times."

Everybody said— "Toi! Toi!!" in agreement.

xxx

The work of dismantling continued.
But, not feeling well, Arniko stopped working.
He hobbled home with the help of Liu.

As he lay down on the bed,
He felt the pain in his right leg becoming unbearable.
Still, he thought he had only a sprain.

Later, he realized that he had high fever.
He became sick.
He didn't have any appetite for the evening meal.

Liu asked— "Teacher, need to see a doctor?"

Arniko said— "Let it be for tonight."

xxx

Late in the midnight,
Delirious Arniko suddenly rose and said—
"Oh mom, where are you?"

His wife embraced him tightly in despair and asked—
"What's the matter?
No one came here."

He sighed remembering his home.
Then said holding her hands—
"A moment ago my mom came here and asked—
'My son! My child!! What happened to your leg?'

"But, I could not speak up.

"She put wine and medicine in my leg and asked—
'Son, when are you returning home?'

"Still, I could not talk.

"Then, she vanished before my eyes."

The wife said in a serious tone—
"Don't know what actually this dream is!
Things are seen as if in reality.
The eyes are closed but the things are seen clearly.
Who knows if someone is hiding inside and watching?"

Arniko thought—
"This is a logical question,
To search for oneself in nothingness."

He said—

"Who taught you to talk like this?

Tell me frankly all about this."

She said frankly— "Sister Miao Yen did."

Puzzled, Arniko questioned— "Sister Miao Yen?"

She repeated— "Yes, Sister Miao Yen."

While he was being overwhelmed by the past memories,

She continued—

"I had entered the palace, two years back.

Sister Miao Yen used to tell me stories about Sakyamuni.

"Later, my auntie knew about this and she got angry.

Don't know why!

She separated me from her,

And sent here as a bride."

Arniko understood the case.

His mind fluctuated,

Like water drops rolling back and forth on a lotus leaf.

xxx

Next morning,

Arniko tried to get to his feet.

But, he could not stand up straight.

He was crippled.

Later in the day,

Two imperial physicians arrived.

Physician Chao examined the leg.
And, punctured five needles and said—
"Gentleman, don't worry.
It is just a sprain.
Will be alright after three doses of acupuncture."

The other, Physician Kaw, examined his pulse and said—
"Gentleman,
This fever is due to the pain in the leg.
There is no reason to be worried.

"You are overburdened in the construction of the White Dagoba.
But your work is unique and historic.
The Emperor is very much pleased with your deeds.

"This tonic was prepared by the order of His Majesty,
For consumption by His Majesty himself.
But, now, His Majesty has ordered to give it to you.

"This is Neku Bhasma.
Take it regularly with this ginseng.
It will redouble your strength."

Arniko queried about the man he had rescued—
"Someone taking care of the friend who fell down?
Even though he has no cuts, he may be in great pains."

Both of them looked sharply at Arniko,
And commented in one voice—
"This is an unnecessary worry."

Without waiting for any response,
They got up and left, saying— "Well, we are leaving."

Arniko conscientiously talked to himself—
"In fact, this White Dagoba belongs to all.
I didn't construct it alone.
Nor did I complete it alone.

"Hundreds of devoted workers,
Who have faith in Buddha, Dharma and Sangha,
Have sweated blood over this project.

"I must report this to the Emperor.
Otherwise, history will blame me very selfish."

Next moment, he changed his mind and said—
"What if the Emperor gets annoyed with my words?
He may tell me to go back to Nepal.

"Well, that's not bad.
I'm not scared to return to my own country.
But, I can't disregard the co-operation of the devoted workers."

While he was talking to himself like this,
His wife, just back from outside, asked—
"Why are you murmuring?
I heard you mentioned Nepal."

Arniko does not know hiding of the facts.
Said frankly—
"Well girl, will you come with me if I go back to Nepal?"

May be, she was curious to see Nepal.
She answered—

"Even if you don't take me there,
I will follow you as your own shadow."

She then sat down with a despairing sigh.

xxx

Arniko is gradually recovering from his pain in the leg.
He started strolling with the help of a walking stick.

One day, amidst rising appetite out of his recovery,
He desired to taste Wo.
So, he asked his wife to buy some Maye.
But she bought Moo instead.

Realizing, Moo Wo is better nourishing than Maye Wo,
He explained how to cook Wo.

After a good try,
She brought two pieces of bread, freshly out of frying pan.
Each piece was oily at one side,
And slightly charred at the other side.

Arniko, who expected delicious Wo, tasted Marpa instead.

He slowly looked at her face and laughed sarcastically.

Ashamed, she bent down her head and murmured—
"The hand made to cook dumplings was asked to cook Wo.
And, I tried my best.
Why make so much fun out of this?"

Instantly, Arniko comforted— "Sorry, my fault."

Some other day,
Well-recovered Arniko, in his workplace, had a new idea.

The Nepalese tradition is that—
On either side of Sakyamuni in a monastery,
Sariputra and Maudagalyan are displayed.

But he decided to display Anand and Kasyap instead,
Following the Chinese tradition.
And, he thoughtfully shaped wax moulds for such images.

Something was still going on in his mind.
He looked into mirror and kept on smiling surprisingly.
The idea behind was that—
Once again he wanted another image.

It was the image of Milapu—
The Chinese version of Maitrya Bodhisatwa.

Milapu is fat, potbellied and always smiling.
An image of Milapu, fingering rosary and greeting all the visitors,
Can be found at the entrance of every monastery in China.

xxx

Liu entered with two nuns.
Both Arniko and his wife welcomed them courteously.
They were seated.

Nun Wei spoke waving a colorful fan—

"Gentleman, we have come here with a purpose.
We came towards Fa Yu Yan Monastery on an official mission,
From Than Cha Sa Monastery.
Miss Miao Yen has given us a task to visit here.

"Our monk colleagues also have told us repeatedly,
Not to return without paying a visit to the White Dagoba,
Under construction here."

She opened her purse,
Took out two bars of pure gold and added—
"Miss Miao Yen has sent this.

"One bar is for gilding the images.
She has told, you will understand at the spell of,
Buddha, Dharma and Sangha.

"The next bar is dedicated to the skills of your hands."

Mention of Miao Yen,
Reminded Arniko, once again, of the days past.

His wife inquired—
"How is Sister Miao Yen? Is she well?
When will she be coming here?"

Chu, the other nun said—
"May be, she won't come here in the near future.
She has already changed her mind."

Liu inquired—
"Isn't she the daughter of our Emperor?"

Nun Wei answered—
"Yes gentleman, yes.
But now,
She is going to become a member of Association of Nuns."

Arniko's wife asked—
"Why so?"

Chu replied quickly—
"To search oneself."

Arniko's wife added—
"I didn't understand what you said."

Chu explained—
"The fact is like this—
It is just like saying,
Something, which does not exist, is in existence.

"If we look for it,
We can't find it.

"For example, an oil-lamp.
It is based on—
Oil, thread, and the name 'oil-lamp' itself.

"Without them, there is no term like oil-lamp.

"Likewise, no one is separate from body, mind and name.
This is what we mean,
By 'searching oneself in nothingness'."

Arniko's wife shook her head in confusion.

108

On the contrary,
Arniko is visualizing skin, blood, bones etc. in his own body.

Further, he is visualizing,
Molecules and atoms in the skin.

Similarly,
He is visualizing his own mind as composed of,
Momentary thoughts, views and feelings.

That again is composed of,
Minute particles of molecules and atoms,
Or, proton, neutron and electrons.

Then, the molecules and atoms were lost into nothingness.
Amidst the nothingness, there was the silence of emptiness.

Dismantling of scaffold,
Around the one-hundred-and-eight-Hand's tall White Dagoba,
Is complete.

Flow of visitors is seen in plenty as usual.

Emperor Hu Pi Le himself has turned up cheerfully,
On horseback,
To have full view of this White Dagoba.

He is followed by Chi Shi,
An old scholar on religion, holding the position of,
The Chief of the Department of Religious Affairs.

At the very sight of the majestic view,
From a bit distant place,
The emperor was fascinated.

Continuing their advance towards the spot,
He told Chi Shi—
"My efforts to develop this Da Du into a metropolis,
And the new capital of greater China,
Has come to perfection now.

"You are also a learned man.
What do you say?"

Chi Shi put forward his idea in tune with the emperor's mood—
"Your Majesty, allow me to say something,
About the historical background, first."

The emperor stroked his goatee reflectively and said—
"Go ahead."

Chi Shi went on saying—
"Of course, Hermit Khun Mun Chu,
The contemporary of Sakyamuni,
Too had come up with a new philosophy.

"But, he failed to talk about religion.

"Later, Hermit Lao Che propounded Taoism.
But, this religion, too, could not spread.

"With the rise of the Han Dynasty,
Buddhism entered from the south,
Moved towards the north,
And began to spread here and there in this country.

"All the peace loving people,
Adopted Buddhism from the core of their heart.

"Three ruling dynasties in succession,
Conferred royal honor on this religion.

"During the period of six other succeeding dynasties,
This religion flourished,
And spread like sunshine, all over the country.

"However,
Sometime later in this very country,
During the reign of Chin Dynasty,
An unprecedented misfortune swept over this religion.

"Emperor Thai Woo,
Acting on the advice of his notorious minister,
Tried to strike covertly and overtly against this religion.

"Yet, withstanding all the misfortunes and obstacles,
This true religion of Buddhism,
Emerged testified and purified.

"Later, during the period of Tang Dynasty,
This religion, together with art and culture,
Flourished to peak level.

"Now,
In this period of rise of Yuan Dynasty,
By grace of Your Majesty the great admirer of religion,
Arniko, a great artist from Nepal,
Has built this superb White Dagoba.

"It is big, tall and unique.
It has the combination of art, religion and philosophy.
This is the greatest contribution of this age.

"Its impact will be seen on the social life of our people—
In their thinking, attitude and behavior.

"Certainly,
Its impact on art, culture, and tradition,
Will last for many decades to come."

The emperor said—
"You are right. I have the same idea."

Chi Shi added—
"In this context, we have to look back a bit.
We have to remember the great monks,
Fa Shi Yan and Huan Tsang who set out in quest of relics;
Made pilgrimages;

"And paid homage to Lumbini where Lord Buddha was born.

"Likewise,
We have to remember Sue Sian,
Who came here from Kapilvastu,
As a living encyclopedia of Buddhism.

"Further, we have to remember the Nepalese bride Chi Chen,
Who crossed the Himalayas carrying Buddhism as her dowry.

"And now,
Today, this sky-high holy White Dagoba,
Is blooming like an immortal lotus flower,
In the garden of Yuan Dynasty."

Amidst such conversation,
The emperor and Chi Shi strolled around the White Dagoba.
And, appreciated it repeatedly.

Arniko was standing right in front of them.

The emperor asked about the monastery,
To be built in perfect harmony with the White Dagoba—
"Gentleman,
What about Da Shang Wan An Monastery?
When will you start, and when will it be complete?"

Arniko explained gesturing with his hands—
"Special timber from Santung has already arrived.
Images of Tathagat Buddha in different styles,
Are being carved.
I won't stay idle just because the White Dagoba is complete.

"The work is going on continuously.
I won't stop the work."

The emperor further inquired—
"When shall we add life to this White Dagoba?
I got a message that,
Teacher Pasapa has already left Lhasa."

Arniko took out Patro from his pocket,
Checked dates for a moment and said—
"Coming Pragya Day is the most suitable day.
This is the day when Sakyamuni became Buddha."

The emperor said –
"Alright. That's fine!", and left.

xxx

Pragya Day,
The day when Sakyamuni became Buddha,
Is coming nearer and nearer.
Teacher Pasapa, too, has arrived in Da Du.

Seeing the superb and majestic White Dagoba,
Pasapa gladly said to Arniko—
"I took you here in Da Du with great hope.
Today, my hope is fulfilled."

Arniko said politely—
"All this has become possible by grace of you,
The Great Teacher."

The name and fame of the White Dagoba,
Continued to spread in all directions.

One day,
A famous poet known as Chang Chu Fu,
Came to pay a visit to the White Dagoba,
In order to see the facts with his own eyes.

Having had seen with poet's eyes,
Right on the spot,
He composed a poem in Ru Meng Ling style.

Then he met with Arniko and expressed—
"Nepalese Gentleman,
Your White Dagoba has surpassed my pride.

"I don't want to talk too much.
But, I would like to show you a poem,
That I just composed.

"Many things still remain inside my heart.
So, I will be coming to see you again and again."

Arniko was at a loss what to say.
After reading the poem he said—
"Sir, now I recognized you."

xxx

Some other day,
Renowned artist Chou Meng Fu led a group of disciples.
And, visited there.

The very sight of the White Dagoba made his skilful hand,
Impatient with excitement.

But, first he told his disciples—
"Take up your positions anywhere you like.
Study this White Dagoba through external and internal eyes.
Then paint its exact picture in the individual styles.

"Remember,
It shall be a test,
Whether your minds are as sharp as the skills of your hands."

The disciples acknowledged in one voice,
And proceeded to take up positions of their choice.

Impatient Chou Meng Fu himself,
Looking at the White Dagoba carefully,
Readied different colors for his work to start.

Reciting Namsangiti, Arniko happened to come.
Two eminent artists exchanged cordial smiles.

Finally,
The renowned artist finished his painting work.
In this picture with vast blue background,
The White Dagoba looked excellent,
Like a white lotus flower in full bloom.

xxx

Some other day,
The group leader of a delegation of monks,
From Wu Thai San Monastery in Sansi Province,

Introduced himself to Arniko and made a request—
"Nepalese Gentleman,
Have your good will on the holy highland,
Of Five Towering Peaks,
Where Maha Manjushree Bodhisatwa once resided.

"Please build another Dagoba like this, over there.
This is a humble request from all of us."

At the very spell of Maha Manjushree,
Arniko recited a prayer in rhythmic voice.
And said—
"I have the same wish.
I will certainly come to Wu Thai San."

xxx

The fabulous news about the White Dagoba,
Reached Lang Feng district in Hanan Province,
Crossing the Hu Pe Province.

Renowned astronomer and mathematician there,
Sir Kuo Sau Ching,
Decided to carry out a survey on it.

On a special day, selected astrologically,
He led a group of disciples,
With all the necessary equipments on their back.

Upon the arrival,
A camp was set up and all the equipments were put into order.
Then the survey work progressed, night and day.

The camp itself is gathering crowds,
Out of the visitors to the White Dagoba.
They were puzzled to see what was going on over there.

Kuo Sau Ching has already filled up many sheets of paper,
With lines and data.

Arniko, too, was drawn towards the center of the crowd,
Out of curiosity what's going on over there!

Kuo Sau Ching asked—
"Is it true, this White Dagoba was built by a Nepalese?"

He nodded—
"Yes. But, why?"

Kuo Sau Ching said—
"The man who built this White Dagoba,
Is not only an architect,
He should be an astronomer too.

"The angles, triangles, and the rectangles, as well as,
The curves, semicircles and the circles in this White Dagoba,
Are all in proportion and symmetry.

"Each of them and the Chhatra above the Chakrabali,
Are all very symbolic, from the astronomical point of view.

"Viewed from any side or any position,
The middle portion is always seen rounded.

"Viewed from anywhere, its shadow is never seen.

"The tinkling of the bells around the Chhatra,
Is proportionately related,
To the direction and the speed of wind.

"It may be able to tell the occurrence of,
Storms, thunderstorms or cyclones,
And the direction from which they come,
As well as their intensity.

"It may even predict,
The occurrence of an earthquake and its intensity.

"I am trying to derive some mathematical relationship.
So that—
The data of sound from these bells,
May predict and measure the above mentioned,
Meteorological and geographical phenomena."

In the meantime,
Siberian and Mongolian cold wind approached from the north,
Whining and gusting every now and then.
That kept Kuo Sau Ching quite busy in noting down the data,
Related to the sound produced by the bells.

Arniko, who had been listening attentively to him, thought—
"This is a learned scholar."

A desire grew within him,
To establish intimate friendship with Kuo Sau Ching.

On the other hand,
Kuo Sau Ching was still ignorant of the fact that,
He had been talking to Arniko.

(In new clothes tailored by his wife,
He looked like a local resident of Da Du.
Nobody would regard him a foreigner, at the first sight.)

He said frankly—
"I wanted to ask one question with the man,
Who designed this White Dagoba."

Arniko inquired without disclosing his identity—
"What is that question?"

Kuo Sau Ching said—
"Considered from the astronomical point of view,
The make up of the universe is such that,
It has only nine stages.

"But here, I find thirteen stages.
I don't understand on what basis it is so.

"So,
I am looking forward to meet the gentleman called Arniko,
Who designed and built this White Dagoba.
And, talk about this with him in detail."

Arniko was now in such an embarrassing circumstance,
It was becoming much too unfair, not to disclose his identity.

But he could not speak up.
Instead, he took out from his inner pocket,
The red sealed certificate of his designation 'Ta Sa Thu'.
That was conferred on him by Emperor Hu Pi Le.
He showed it to Kuo Sau Ching.

After reading this certificate,
Kuo Sau Ching said—
"Great! Gentleman Arniko, I have a request.
I have a big plan to build an observatory.
I need your help.
What is your idea?"

Arniko replied happily—
"All my knowledge and all my skill,
Whatever I have, belong to all."

Pragya Day,
The day when Sakyamuni became Buddha,
Has finally come.

The White Dagoba is religiously decorated.
Beautiful welcome-gates are erected.
Multicolored buntings are fluttered.

Early from the dawn,
People started crowding towards the White Dagoba—
Some playing devotional music;
Some reciting prayers;
Some offering flowers;
Some offering Gulpa pots;
Some carrying censers filled with frankincense;
And, some burning incense sticks in their hands.

Some are orbiting the White Dagoba devotionally.
Some have done so already,
And are busing themselves in groups.

Tiny bells fitted on costumes of the Lion Dancers,
Jingled in tune with drums and cymbals,
To the amusement of every ones.

Street hawkers are having their time too.
Candy and cakes to toys,
Silk and velvet clothes to costume jewelry,
Are on sell.

Some are having a look.
Some are buying.
And, some are just bargain hunting.

xxx

Spectators cheered into roaring voices,
At the arrival of Emperor Hu Pi Le.

He is followed by a galaxy of fair ladies and brave knights.

Arniko and his colleagues,
Welcomed the emperor with garlands and bouquets.

Amidst rituals,
The task of adding life to the White Dagoba,
Is formally accomplished as per time honored traditions.

Emperor Hu Pi Le extended his hands,
And humbly accepted a sweet smelling flower—
Symbolic of super-blessing.

He smelt it with devotion.
Then he proclaimed—
"Now onwards,
This White Dagoba,
Has formally become an embodiment of Bodhi Chita!

"It is strictly forbidden to do any harm on it!"

Having said this,
He held crown-like caps one by one,
And put them on the heads of Arniko,
And other chiefs of the skilled workers.

Each of them were garlanded with embroidered Pa Pau,
And muffled up in beautiful scarves too.

Also,
A pouch of coins was given as cash prize to each of them.

Next,
The emperor generously announced a dinner party,
In their recognition.

After that,
The emperor, following the Mongol tradition,
Let two pairs of cute deer to go free,
As offerings to the White Dagoba.

Overjoyed Arniko spoke—
"Friends!
These prizes from the farsighted savior of the religion,
Emperor Hu Pi Le,
Belong to each of us,
Engaged in the construction of this White Dagoba.

"Next, the two pairs of deer!
Let each of us be capable to keep them up.
So that—
This religious spot may be thought of,
As a religious Deer Park, too.

"Moreover,
We have to plant oak, pine and Chusa trees all around here.
Then, the periphery of this White Dagoba,
Will have clean and fresh atmosphere."

Cheers and joys filled the air, time and again.
Trained deer raised their heads to look at the White Dagoba.

The emperor suggested—
"Teacher,
On this pious occasion of adding life to the White Dagoba,
A few religious words from you,
Shall purify our mind."

While Pasapa readied himself to begin his religious talk,
People moved closer to listen.

Volunteers shouted—
"Silence! Silence!!
Please stay where you are and listen quietly!"

Slowly the situation came back to normal.

After praying to the White Dagoba for a moment,
Pasapa preached to the large crowds—
"I am unable to fully describe,
The significance of this White Dagoba.
So, I will say something as I know and as I can.

"Erected on Bhupur Mandala,
This White Dagoba is a symbol of,
International Brotherhood and World Peace!

"Emerging above a fully bloomed lotus flower,
This White Dagoba is a true symbol of Buddhism!

"Having a large belly, covered with Pindapatra,
This White Dagoba is an embodiment of,
Incomparable knowledge of Parmarthagyan!

"Its multistoried Chakrabali,
With thirteen concentric circles,
Representing Thirteen Heavens,
Is an embodiment of mastery of all religions!

"Its summit,
Over the Dharma Chhatra in the form of Purna Kalas,
Is symbolic of the crown of all the Buddha's.

"In summation,
Filled with every pious qualities,
This White Dagoba is a symbol of,
The Light of Swayembhu!

"To think of it,
To concentrate on it,
And to orbit it,
Are all the mediums of converting one's Chita,
Into Bodhi Chita through Nirbikalpa Samadhi.

"One thing,
When we surrender ourselves to Buddha, Dharma and Sangha,
It is not sufficient to consider only the past or the future events.
It is most necessary to consider the present event.

"What is going on in one's Chita, now?
It should be studied, understood and realized.

"One should learn to look at oneself and know oneself.

"The state of one's Chita!
What are affecting it and what the effects are!
They should all be analyzed.

"In other words,
Life is not just to survive.
We must free our Chita from Klais.

"We must control our Chita,
Like the bridling of a horse,
Or, like the driving of an elephant by a mahout.

"There are so many things to tell.
It is just not possible to tell them all.
So, let me tell you a simple but meaningful story.

Once,
During the days of Sakyamuni,
An old hunchback went to a monastery,
Hoping to learn Buddhism.

But he could not grasp anything,
No matter how much the monk scholars explained him.

They told him—
"Your head is like a clay pot with cracks.
It can't be filled."

Frustrated,
The old man decided to commit suicide,
By jumping into a river.

Somehow, Sakyamuni came to know about this.
He sent messengers to take the old man to his hermitage.

Sakyamuni urged—

"Studying hard or meditations are not compulsory,
To learn my religion.
So, I tell you to do one thing.

"Take a broom and go to a Stupa anywhere,
And sweep the place clean of dusts.

"Remember one thing!
You have to clean thoroughly,
By clearing all kinds of dust or rubbish.

"This much is your daily task.
Keep on doing it perfectly."

As advised by Sakyamuni,
Everyday, he visited a Stupa,
And dedicated him in cleaning work.

Buds of Pragya
Started burgeoning inside the heart of the old man,
Who once wanted to die.

One day,
He found the truth,
While searching him within himself.

He said to himself—
"Dust and dirt are lying, not only on the outside.
They are accumulated inside my Chita too,
In the form of Klais.

"The reason,
Why Sakyamuni told me to keep on doing cleaning work is that,

128

"The dust and dirt accumulated inside me must be cleaned up."

Later on,
As the old man became successful in his Charya,
His Chita developed into Bodhi Chita.

Ultimately,
Scenes of attainment of Bodhigyan by Sakyamuni,
By meditating under the Bodhi Tree,
Flashed right in front of his eyes in a systematic order.

He came to understand the facts,
About the Four Truths and their significance.

He thoroughly understood Panchaskandha.

Further, he came to realize that—
Each branch of any philosophy is so deep,
Whereas a man's life, so short.

And that—
The ideas of Sakyamuni and his holy words,
Have shown the simplest and shortest route to Bodhigyan.

Finally,
Ye Dharma Hetu Prabhava flourished inside him,
Like a lotus flower,
That does not get wet,
Even though it emerges out of water.

"That is the story.
Ten directions! Three time periods!
May goodness and happiness come to all!"

Everybody vowed in one voice—
"We will follow Tri Ratna."

xxx

Bright full moon is rising above the Pohai Sea in the east.

The golden summit of the White Dagoba,
Lit brilliantly under the moonlight,
Is seen clearly from all directions.

It is illuminating like a beacon-light of Prabhaswar.

The tinkling of the bells around the Dharma Chhatra,
Is producing the melodies of Pragya and Punya.

Considering it as Bodhi Chita,
Everyone is praying,
To the White Dagoba with great devotion.

Everyone is experiencing peaceful comfort,
From the rays of friendship and kindness,
Radiating out from the White Dagoba.

xxx

Salient White Dagoba,
An everlasting gift of Arniko,
Stood prominently,
As an embodiment of Bodhi Chita of Sakyamuni Buddha.
And, as a symbol of Swayembhu Jyoti.

Many years passed.

One day,
At the age of sixty two,
Arniko was bedridden.

When medicines did not work,
He realized his time had come.

He was aware of the fact that,
Death is an unbreakable law of nature.

So, he put his Chita attached to the White Dagoba.

His Pragya met with Prabhaswar,
Embodied in the Chita Chaitanya.

Yethayen Aagat Tathagat,
Was standing right in front of him.

Finally, saying 'Tri Ratna Saran' to his last breath,
He departed from this world,
Leaving behind his mortal body.

His wives and children,
Remained in the observance of mourning rituals.

Everyone who came to console the bereaved family said—
"Nowhere can we find another artist of his talent and skill."

The mourning rituals were performed,
As per traditions of the countries,
Where he was born as well as where he resided.

His dead body was buried with full military honor,
In Kang Che Yuan of Sian Shan Thum,
That lies in Wan Ping district, west of Da Du metropolis.

Later,
Emperor Woo Sung,
Honoring his invaluable qualities and contributions,
Posthumously conferred on him,
The title of Kong Khai Fu Yu Sa Shan Sa Thai Sa,
As well as the title of Ming Hui.

Further,
As ordered by the emperor,
All the facts and figures about Arniko were compiled.

And,
His biography was engraved,
On a monumental pillar,
Decorated with images of dragons.

The monumental pillar was erected,
Above the back of a stone tortoise,
At the burial site.

All this and that helped,
To keep Arniko's memory long lasting,
For many centuries.

Poor or rich,
Foolish or wise,
Whoever comes,
Has all to go.

Centuries after their departure,
Only a few are remembered.

And, only a few creations of the few so remembered,
Might still be in existence—
Shining like the stars.

One such prominent star is—
The White Dagoba in Beijing, China.

Witnessed by history,
The White Dagoba has withstood,
Thousands of storms and thunderstorms.

No doubt, this is a masterpiece of Arniko—
The architect hero of Nepal.

This is also a symbol of friendship and co-operation,
Between Nepal and China.

Pages to follow are my endeavor at this old age,
To appreciate,
Arniko, and his marvelous creations.

(This page is the preface of the original book)

ARNICO'S ARCHITECTURAL LEGACY

"Seven centuries ago, a 17-years-old Nepalese artisan named Arnico climbed over the Himalayas, crossed the Yellow River and came to Beijing, then called Dadu (Great Capital). He went to work for the Yuan Dynasty (1271-1368) court and died in China.

Today's Beijing would be unrecognizable to Arnico; but he would see at least one familiar sight— the White Dagoba he designed in the city's western district. One of the oldest standing structures in the city, it remains a striking feature of Beijing's skyline despite 700 years of erosion by wind and rain.

Yuan Dynasty records describe Arnico as an accomplished architect, painter, sculptor and mechanical engineer. He is among the few foreigners whose biography can be found in Chinese imperial history books. The White Dagoba was built under his supervision from 1271 to 1279. Renovated in 1980, it is now open to tourists."

—Hai Lan; CHINA DAILY; Saturday, October 3, 1981

(Extract from the original book)

GLOSSARY

Add life— To inaugurate with religious procedures.

Ambasha— A part of a Dagoba or Stupa.

Amitabha— Buddha.

Anand— He became an Arahat under the teachings of Buddha.

Arahat— One of the five hundred advanced disciples of Buddha.

Arniko (1244-1306)— The Nepalese hero who crossed the Himalayas more than 700 years ago, designed and built many masterpieces in China and settled there.

A Newar from Kathmandu Valley, he led a group of 80 Nepalese artists to Tibet. Impressed by his skills, he was taken to Beijing (then Da Du) where he designed and built the White Dagoba (Miao Ying Temple or Bai Ta). Built in 8 years (1271-79) it was designated a historical treasure after the founding of the People's Republic of China.

Ta Sa Thu (equivalent of a minister) and many other titles were conferred on him by different emperors. He was honored even after his death. He is among the few foreigners whose biography is found in Chinese imperial history books.

He had 11 wives, 10 of them Chinese. Out of his 6 sons and 7 daughters, 1 son and 1 daughter were from the Nepalese wife. Both of them were married to Chinese better halves.

Issuance of Nepalese postage stamp with his portrait; designation of a Himalayan peak (6034 meters) as Arniko Peak; and naming of the Nepal-China road as Arniko Highway are some of the positive steps in his commemoration.

Arye Namsangiti— Namsangiti. A hymn for Pragyaparmita.

Astasahastrika Pragyaparmita— A voluminous book on Pragyaparmita.

Avlokiteswar—Bungadyo. A Bodhisatwa.

Bajra Yan— A branch of Buddhism.

Basundhara's Sinhamhu— A saffron-pot used in religious rituals.

Bhrikuti— Daughter of king Amsubarma (588-635) of Nepal married to Sran Chang Gempo. She is worshipped as a Tara.

Bhupur Mandala— A special type of mandala symmetrically bordered by 20 salient angles and 16 reentering angles formed by 36 sides of different length in the ratio 1:4:12. Each of the four directions has nine sides— one longest side in the middle, two sides of medium length and two sides of shortest length on either side of this longest side. The shortest sides join the other sides including the longest side at right angles.

Bodhi— Intelligence or knowledge by which one becomes a Buddha or a believer in Buddhism. Buddha.

Bodhi Chita— Noble desire to attain Bodhi.

Bodhigyan— Knowledge on Bodhi.

Bodhipad— The status of Buddha.

Bodhi Parinamana Chita— Arrival at Bodhi Chita.

Bodhi Pranidhi Chita— Determination to have Bodhi Chita.

Bodhi Prasthan Chita— Departure towards Bodhi Chita.

Bodhisatwa— A Buddha at pre-Nirvana state.

Bodhi Tree— The tree under which Sakyamuni did seven years' penance, and under which he became Buddha.

Buddha— Intelligent person ready to enter Nirvana.

There are Buddha's of the past, present and future. Most popular one is the Sakyamuni Buddha born 2,551 years ago as a crown prince in Lumbini, Nepal.

Bunga— A spot in Yela with a temple of Bungadyo.

Bungadyo— A popular god whose chariot is pulled around Yela and celebrated every year as a festival.

Chakrabali— The upper portion of a Dagoba with thirteen concentric circles.

Chang Ah— Chinese fable goddess who reached the moon, carrying wine having immortalizing power. (Chinese term)

Chang An— Old capital of China, location not same as Beijing. (Chinese term)

Chaosan— Korea. (Chinese term)

Charya— Religious practices.

Chautara— A place to take rest under a pair of trees (Ber and Pipal).

Chhatra— Dharma Chhatra.

Chiao Che— Vietnam. (Chinese term)

Chi Chen— Bhrikuti. (Chinese term)

Chisya— A pundit on religion. (Chinese term)

Chita— Mind. State of mind. Desire.

Chita Chaitanya— Mind and soul.

Chung Du— Beijing before Yuan Dynasty. (Chinese term)

Chun-jie— New Year Spring Festival. (Chinese term)

Chusa— A kind of tree. (Chinese term)

Chyampati— Stone of a small fleshy sour fruit (Chaeospondeaz oxilaris).

Daanam Bibhusanam— Charity is one of the noblest qualities of a man.

Da Du— Beijing during Yuan Dynasty. Meaning is Great Capital. (Chinese term)

Dagoba— A dome shaped structure symbolic of Buddhism. Stupa.

Da Shang Wan An Monastery— Monastery for longevity and protection of the emperor. (Chinese term)

Day of washing-hair— One of the activities of a marriage ceremony.

Dharma— Religion. Buddhism.

Dharma Chhatra— Umbrella shaped part of a Dagoba or Stupa.

Disciple-friend— Disciple treated as a friend.

Elixir-wine— Wine having immortalizing power.

Even a small Chyampati can ... ...— Small things can do great job.

Even a sparrow in your house ... ...— Excessive privacy maintained.

Face-looking-day— One of the activities of a marriage ceremony.

Fa Kwa— A masked artist.

Fi Kwa— A masked artist.

Fish, Parrots, Aintha, Joprasad— Varieties of bread.

Five Sister Mountains— Wu Thai San.

Five Towering Peaks— Wu Thai San.

Fluctuated like water drops rolling back and forth ... ...— Confused.

Four Truths— See page 52 (4th paragraph).

Fu Che Men— A gate by this name.

Gadh... ...; Kuti; Jhikhachhen; Tingri Plains— Landmarks en route.

Ganesh Himal— Snow-capped mountain by this name.

God of the Door— Self explanatory.

God of the House— Self explanatory.

God of the Kitchen— Self explanatory.

God of Skills— Self explanatory.

God of Works— Self explanatory.

Golden Stupa— Stupa by this name.

Gridhakut— The hermitage in India where Buddha talked about Maha Yan.

Gulpa— A pot to fill with cereals offered to Buddha.

Haaw— Good. (Chinese term)

Hand— Length from elbow to tip of middle finger. (2 Hand's = 1 yard)

Hridayasutra— Pragyaparmita Hridayasutra.

Huang Tsang— Chinese pilgrim who visited Lumbini in 633 A.D.

Hu Pi Le (1215-1294)— Founder of Yuan Dynasty. He assigned Arniko to build the White Dagoba. Also called Kublai Khan / Sa Chu. (Chinese term)

Hyese— Abbot. (Chinese term)

Jhomolongmo— The Mount Everest.

Jung Chew Jie— A festival by this name. (Chinese term)

Kang— Bed, smoke-warmed from underneath.

Kapilvastu— Forest nearby Lumbini.

Karunamaya…— Bungadyo.

Kasyap— A disciple of Buddha, after whose death he convoked and acted as chairman of the first synod.

Khasti— Bouddhanath Stupa, Kathmandu.

Khensagun— Serving hard boiled then fried whole egg, fried small whole fish, and small pieces of fried meat put over Wo in one hand and wine in the other hand. Religious practice of wishing success or congratulating.

Khotan— A town by this name. (Chinese term)

Klais— Dirt. Dirt in the mind.

Kwan Yin— Bodhisatwa. (Chinese term)

Kwe— Measure word of distance (about 2 miles).

Land of Buddha— Lumbini.

Lhasa— Capital of Tibet.

Li— Measure word of distance. (Chinese term)

Light of Swayembhu— Divinely rays radiating from Swayembhu.

Like a monkey fallen down from a tree— A monkey that slips down from a tree is believed to be disgraced.

Lion Dancers— Self explanatory.

Lion of Yuan Dynasty— Hu Pi Le.

Liu / Liu Yuan— Arniko's disciple who rose to a high position. (Chinese term)

Living Goddess— Kumari, a virgin girl worshipped as goddess.

Loknath— Bungadyo.

Lokpal— An associate god.

Lotus— Flower of symbolic significance in Buddhism.

Lu Kou Chew— Stone bridge in Beijing nearby Arniko's burial site. Known as Marco Polo Bridge these days. (Chinese term)

Lumbini— The birthplace of Buddha.

Madhyamik Darshan— A school of thought on Buddhism.

Maha Manjushree…— Manjushree.

Maha Yan— A branch of Buddhism.

Maitrya Bodhisatwa— A Bodhisatwa by this name.

Mangal Dhoon— Religious tune wishing success.

Manjeswari Hill— The hill with the image of Manjushree beside Swayembhu Stupa in Kathmandu.

Manjushree…— She came to Nepal from Wu Thai San in China as a Bodhisatwa. Kathmandu Valley then was a huge lake. She cut pieces of land with an axe to drain off the lake and made the valley fit for settlement. She is worshiped as a powerful goddess.

Marco Polo— Italian traveler who served Yuan Dynasty for seventeen years. A stone bridge in Beijing is famous these days as Marco Polo Bridge.

Satya Mohan Joshi, in his another book on Arniko, has hypothesized that Marco Polo and Arniko must have met each other sometime during the construction of the White Dagoba. Considered the travel accounts of Marco Polo, the hypothesis may be plausible.

Marpa— A kind of bread.

Maudagalyan— Left-hand attendant disciple of Buddha.

Maye— A pulse bean.

Maye Wo— Salty bread made of Maye.

Men Tian— Burma. (Chinese term)

Middle path— A branch of Buddhism.

Milapu— A Bodhisatwa. (Chinese term)

Mongo Fa Thing— A meeting hall by this name. (Chinese term)

Moo— Kidney bean.

Moo Wo— Salty bread made of Moo.

Mother Chang Ah— Chang Ah.

Mother Saraswati— Saraswati.

Mysterious facts about Nepal— Only 147,181 sq. km. approximately in area, Nepal is remarkable for:

-Diversity of all kinds. Diverse topography, diverse climate, diverse flora and fauna, diverse ethnic groups, diverse complexions, diverse customs, culture and costumes, diverse languages (more than 50), etc.

- 'All climates of the earth: From the tropics to the eternal ice….'- Dietmar Frank

-Mount Everest and other eight highest peaks of the world above 8,000 meters.

-Deepest gorges of the world.

-30 kinds of big wild animals including elephants, tigers, one-horned rhinos, and snow leopards.

-80 kinds of mammals.

-More than 800 species of birds.

-Several hundreds of varieties of butterflies.

-Snowline— 4,572 meters from sea level.

-Eight World Heritage Sites declared by UNESCO.

-Kathmandu Valley: Only 570 sq. km. in area and situated 1,200- 1,500 meters above mean sea level, it has 7 of the 8 World Heritage Sites mentioned above. As late as 236 years ago, the three towns Kantipur, Lalitpur and Bhaktapur of this valley were three small kingdoms.

Na Kwa— Nagarkot, a spot famous for viewing sunrise.

Namaskar— Prayer word.

Namo Amitabha— Prayer word to pray Amitabha.

Namo Ratna Trayayo— Prayer word to pray Ratna Trayayo.

Namsangiti— A hymn for Pragyaparmita.

Nava Ratna— Nine types of precious jewels.

Neku Bhasma— Medicinal ash prepared from horns.

Nepal Bhasa— The mother tongue of Newars of Nepal. Newari.

Nepal Bhasa Parishad— The literary organization that published the original book from which this book in reader's hand has been translated.

Nepal Valley— Kathmandu Valley. Then Nepal. See Mysterious facts… ….

Nepal-ya Rastriye Bibhuti Kalakar Arniko-ya Sweta Chaitya— Title of the original book from which this book in reader's hand has been translated. This title in Nepal Bhasa language means— Nepal's hero, architect Arniko's White Dagoba.

Newar— People of Nepal whose mother tongue is Nepal Bhasa (Newari).

Nirbikalpa Samadhi— Stop breathing. Abstract meditation.

Nirvana— Salvation of soul.

Pa Da Chu Monastery— Ling Quang Monastery in western hills of Beijing. (Chinese term)

Pancha Daan— Five types of charity.

Pancha Rachha— A Buddhist prayer by this name.

Pancharasmi— Divinely rays with five colors.

Panchaskandha— Five instincts (form, perception, consciousness, action, knowledge).

Pa Pau— Garland of sheets with symbols of good luck, e.g. a pair of fish. (Chinese term)

Paramarthagyan— Pragya.

Paru— Day after full moon or new moon.

Pasapa— Emperor Hu Pi Le's teacher on religious matters. (Chinese term)

Patro— Lunar calendar.

Phing Sa Men— Previous name of Fu Cha Men. (Chinese term)

Pindapatra— Bowl to receive alms. The dome of a Dagoba or Stupa looks like an inverted Pindapatra.

Pipal— A kind of tree (Ficus religiosa).

Pohai…— Gulf of Po Hai. (Chinese term)

Potala…— Durbar Square by this name in Lhasa, Tibet. (Chinese term)

Prabhakari— See thirteen heavens.

Prabhaswar— God of light. God of knowledge.

Prabhaswar Swayembhu Jyoti— Swayembhu Jyoti.

Pragya— Knowledge of the illusory character of all existence. Intelligence which leads to Nirvana.

Pragya Day— The day when Buddha attained Buddhaship.

Pragyaparmita— Arrival at the other shore through Pragya. To attain Nirvana. A book on Pragyaparmita.

Pragyaparmita Hridayasutra— Canonical writings on Pragyaparmita.

Pramudita— See thirteen heavens.

Pratityasamutpad— Rudiments of Buddhism. Four Truths.

Punya— The blessings resulting from pious deeds.

Purna Kalas— Jar filled with holy water.

Randy— Lewd.

Ranjana script— The script registered in the United Nations Organization as the main script of Nepal.

Ratna Trayayo— Tri Ratna.

Receiving spot— A spot outside the door where rituals are performed.

Religious-picnic at Ina— One of the activities of a marriage ceremony.

Saka Baha— A monastery by this name.

Sakyabansa— Sakya Dynasty.

Sakya Dynasty— The dynasty of which Buddha was a crown prince.

Sakyamuni…— Buddha.

Samyak— A kind of enlightened knowledge.

Samyak Sambodhigyan— Bodhigyan.

Sangh— Association of Buddhists.

Sangu— A locality by this name.

Sangyanskandha— One of the five instincts. See Panchaskandha.

Sanskarskandha— One of the five instincts. See Panchaskandha.

Saraswati— Mother Saraswati. Goddess prayed for education and skills.

Sariputra— Right-hand attendant and disciple of Buddha.

Satya Mohan Joshi— The author of the original book from which this book in reader's hand has been translated. Born 1920, he is: Life-Member, Literary Academy of Nepal; Chancellor, Nepal Bhasa Academy; Winner, many literary awards.

Sa Yuan Thau— 8th day of the 4th month of Chinese calendar. Birthday of Buddha according to Chinese tradition. (Chinese term)

Serpent God— God of serpents.

Silu Kunda— Gosaikunda, a religious pond at high altitude.

Silu Mye— A folk song which tells the tragic story of a pilgrim to Silu Kunda.

Small feet / Small-footed— Having small feet as a result of hard fashion in then China.

Spring Ceremony— Ceremony held on Sri Panchami.

Sran Chang Gempo— Tibetan emperor with whom Chi Chen (Bhrikuti) and Wen Chen were married.

Srawak Yan— A branch of Buddhism.

Sri Panchami— 1st day of spring season in Nepal. Mother Saraswati is specially worshiped on this day.

Sthiro Wakya— Prayers for firmness and permanency of structures.

Stupa— Dome shaped structure symbolic of Buddhism. Dagoba.

Sun Woo Kung— Chinese legendary monkey who stirred the heaven.

Swayembhu...— Attaining Buddhaship without being taught. A Stupa in Kathmandu by this name.

Swayembhu Jyoti— Light of Swayembhu.

Tantric— Related to supernatural formulae of mystic efficacy.

Tara— Tantric goddess in Buddhist line. Sran Chen Gempo's two wives Chi Chen and Wen Chen are regarded incarnates of Tara and worshipped as White Tara and Green Tara.

Ta Sa Thu—A decoration equivalent of a minister in then China. (Chinese term)

Tathagat...— Buddha.

Ten directions— East, West, North, South, Northeast, Northwest, Southeast, Southwest, Heaven (high above the surface of the earth), and Hell (deep below the surface of the earth).

Thai Su— Mongolian warlord Chen Gez Khan. (Chinese term)

Thiasafu— A religious book with folding pages.

Thirteen Heavens— Buddhism identifies thirteen types of heavens: 1.Pramudita 2.Bimala 3.Prabhakari 4.Archichasmati 5.Sudrarajaya 6.Abhimukhi 7.Durangma 8.Achala 9.Sadhumati 10.Dharma Megha 11.Samanta Prabha 12.Nirupama 13. Gyanbati (Bajrabhumi).

Three time periods— Past, Present and Future

Thufan— Tibet. (Chinese term)

Toi— That is right. (Chinese term)

Tri Bodhi— Tri Ratna.

Tri Bodhi Chita— Inclined to Tri Bodhi.

Tri Ratna— Buddha of the past, present and future. Trinity of precious jewels representing Buddha, Dharma and Sangha.

Tri Ratna Saran— Submission to Tri Ratna.

Twelve-year-anniversary— The anniversary observed in yet grand manner, every twelve years.

Valley— Kathmandu Valley.

Watched the ceiling timbers— dancing!— Day-dreaming.

Wen Chen— Chinese princess married to Sran Chang Gempo. She is worshipped as a Tara. (Chinese term)

White Dagoba— The Bai Ta beside Miao Ying Temple inside Fu Che Men gate. It is 50.9 meters tall and its base is over 30 meters in circumference. It remains a striking feature of Beijing's skyline despite 700 years of erosion by wind and rain. Designed and built by Arniko in eight years (1271-1279), it was designated a historical treasure after People's Republic of China was established.

Wo— Salty bread cooked of crushed bean.

Wu Thai San— Mountain in China from where Manjushree came to Nepal. (Chinese term)

Ye Dharma Hetu Prabhava... ...— A Buddhist epic. See page 12 (2nd and 4th paragraph).

Yela— Lalitpur district. Patan.

Yemraj— God of Death.

Yen Ching— Beijing during Liau Dynasty. (Chinese term)

Yethayen Aagat Tathagat— Buddha.

Yuan Dynasty— The dynasty founded by Emperor Hu Pi Le. (Yuan is Chinese term)

Yue Ye Ping— Crescent shaped special bread of Jung Chew Jie festival. (Chinese term)

Zhen Ziu— Acupuncture. (Chinese term)

BIBLIOGRAPHY

-Hai Lan; Arnico's Architectural Legacy; China Daily, Oct 3, 1981

-Xinhua News Agency; News Bulletin, July2, 1980.

-Macmillan Publishers Ltd, London; The Dictionary of Art, page 477.

-Dietmar Frank; Dreamland Nepal.

-Ernest J. Eitel; A Sanskrit-Chinese Dictionary.

-S.M. Joshi; The Well-Known Nepalese Architect Arniko.

-S.M. Joshi; Bachadhangu Newa Khango Dhuku.

-Ministry of Tourism and Civil Aviation; Visit Nepal 98, The Magnificent Seven

-Sandhya Times; July30, 1997; Debate in the House of Representatives.

-Destination Nepal 1981.

-Travellers' Nepal, July-August, 1999.

-Balchandra Sharma; Nepal-ko Aitihasik Ruprekha

-Dhundiraj Bhandari; Nepal-ko Aitihasik Bibechana

-Surya Bikram Gyawali; Nepal Upatyaka-ko Madhyakalin Itihash

-Dictionary of Contemporary English; Orient Longman Ltd.

-The World Book Dictionary; World Book Inc.

-the thorndike barnhart handy pocket Dictionary; Bantam Books, New York.

-Chandra Lall Singh; Nepali to English Dictionary.

-Nepal Engineers' Association; Diary/Planner 2059.

-New Nepal Press, Kathmandu, Nepal; Calendar 2064 (Bikram Sambat era).

Printed in the United States
By Bookmasters